THE BOX SEAT DRE

A Baseball Story

Richard Bosworth

with illustrations by
Joseph V. Cioffi

BOZ
IMAGINEERING, INC.
Boca Raton, Florida

Published by BOZ IMAGINEERING, INC.
2901 Clint Moore Road, Suite 237
Boca Raton, FL 33496
(888) 922-9492
E-mail: bozimagineering@juno.com
http://www.boxseatdream.com

Library of Congress Catalog Card Number: 00-091358
ISBN: 0-9679395-0-X

For My Parents, Rita and Al

*Thank you for providing your children and
grandchildren with a loving environment
where anything is possible.
Thank you for the fireside chats where my imagination
was allowed to grow endlessly.
Thank you for the unconditional encouragement
to live out my dreams.
But most of all, thank you for teaching me
the meaning of loyalty, respect and perseverance.
You have inspired this story.*

Acknowledgements

Addressing any extracurricular activity requires an extraordinary amount of concentration. I do not believe anyone can live a happy, well-balanced life and attempt such an endeavor without the support of others. I am no different. Without the overwhelming support I received from special individuals around me, *The Box Seat Dream* would have always remained a dream.

My wife Christine said to me once in total confidence, "you must write this story." Christine, I truly believe if you had not said those words, I would have never taken pen to paper. Your encouragement has never faulted and your belief in me can never be duplicated. You touch everyone around you by helping to make dreams come true. Your intuition and insight played an invaluable role in shaping the creation process. Without your diligence, *The Box Seat Dream* would never have been brought to market. You made this book a reality. You are my soul mate and partner in life.

A child, no matter how old, always plays an important role in your life when you reach for the stars. Jackie, I only hope that someday my writing may even approach your ability and creativity. You keep me young at heart. You are my sunshine.

My brother David, I cannot believe you actually let me tell you all those stories when we were growing up. Did you really believe our bunk bed was a train cabin and we were minor league ball players going from town to town? Thank you for being my audience and my friend.

Kevin Clouther, a special friend of our family brought his extraordinary literary talent by contributing to the final edit of *The Box Seat Dream*. Kevin, you will undoubtedly leave your mark in 21st century American literature.

And finally, I have been fortunate to have friends review *The Box Seat Dream* throughout its many stages. You all know who you are. I hope you know your feedback was taken seriously. You will see the changes within the story. Thanks for all the help and support.

There is no room in baseball for discrimination.
It is our national pastime and a game for all.

–Lou Gehrig

PROLOGUE

October 26, 1985

April 18, 1923 was a day I will never forget. Yankee Stadium opened its gates for the very first time. I often wonder if anyone realized then what the stadium would really mean. Not just to a sport or to an entire city, but to the millions of people who would pass through its doors in the many years to come.

Through the decades, I've seen many changes to the ballpark and to the New York Yankees. During those years, if I had to identify a time that was the most glorious, I would say it is today.

This ball game was destined by sixty years of Yankee history. Today's game was a tribute to every player who stepped on the field, with or without Yankee pinstripes. Yet its real glory is to the memory of the Yankee greats who would be the most proud: Babe Ruth, Miller Huggins, and of course, the eternal Lou Gehrig. It is their legend that is forever displayed in this stadium and the center field monuments to whom they are dedicated.

July 4, 1939

"Yet, today I consider myself the luckiest man on the face of the earth." As Number Four spoke into the microphone, a thunderous cheer roared through the stadium. Sitting six rows back behind the first base dugout in her special seat, Mrs. Gehrig watched her husband give his final farewell to 62,000 fans of the New York Yankees.

With tears rolling down her face, she looked up to Sam, who stood beside her. The Yankee usher reached to her, offering his arm, which she accepted as he helped her stand to her feet. Together they joined the greatest ovation ever experienced at Yankee Stadium.

"Sam, I should be with Lou on the field. Will you please escort me there?"

Mrs. Gehrig stepped into the aisle and adoringly looked back at her favorite box seat. She placed her gloved hand on the seat and touched the brass numeric plate that read A1-33. As she turned and continued down the aisle, a bright light flashed from the seat's brass plate. The light caught the corner of Sam's eye and he smiled to himself.

Many of the Yankee fans' eyes were fixed upon them as they continued down the stadium steps toward the field. Mrs. Gehrig turned to Sam and softly said, "Thank you for taking such good care of me throughout these recent years."

"It's been my honor," returned Sam.

"Please make me a promise."

"Anything, Mrs. Gehrig. Just you name it."

"Whomever has the pleasure of owning my box seat in the future, please be sure they love baseball and love the New York Yankees as much as you and I do."

"That's a promise I assure you I'll keep."

Hearing Sam's words brought a look of relief over Mrs. Gehrig's face. She took a deep breath and stepped onto the field.

October 21, 1974

"Hey, Mac, give me a hand over here."

"What's that, Mr. Deavers?"

John McNeil was unable to hear his foreman's voice over the sound of the jackhammers, so he walked closer.

Mr. Deavers and Bill Waters were huddled over a stadium seat. They had a large electric wrench and were trying to loosen the bolts that secured the seat to the concrete. Suddenly, Mr. Deavers and Bill went flying backwards. The open end of the wrench broke off and sailed into the air.

"Forget this," yelled Mr. Deavers as he walked away.

John helped Bill to his feet and turned to watch his boss walk briskly onto the ripped-up infield. Most of the construction stopped while the crew listened to Mr. Deavers' instructions.

Bill turned to John and said, "I think repairing the stadium is going to be harder than we thought."

"Good thing we still have until 1976 to complete it," laughed John.

Bill rolled his eyes and both men began to laugh as they joined the crew for the foreman's meeting.

CHAPTER 1

I need to move quickly, Jimmy thought to himself as he ran down the street. Flying around the corner, he found to his surprise a new leaf pile right in front of him. Unable to slow down, Jimmy went straight through it! The three-foot-high pile caused him to stumble as he came out the other side. Catching his balance, he burst into another sprint, this time jumping over the hedges on Mrs. Brown's lawn and clearing the hurdle easily.

He had to get home before Mom had dinner on the table. Those had been her last instructions when he left the house in the morning: "It's not fair to make your family wait, just because you and your friends are playing football at the schoolyard." His mom's words were still ringing in his ears. As Jimmy approached the house he took a deep breath of relief and smiled. It was autumn and the type of day when you could smell Thanksgiving in the air.

Jimmy McNeil lived in Yonkers, New York, a city just north of New York City. Like many eleven-year-olds in New York, Jimmy was a big sports fan. He rooted for all the hometown teams, and was an especially big fan of the New York Yankees. Jimmy's dream was to one day become a professional baseball player and perhaps even wear a Yankee uniform himself.

"Hey, Mom, I'm home," Jimmy yelled as he barreled his way through the front door. "Is dinner ready yet?" "Almost. Hurry and wash up!" his mom ordered from the kitchen.

Jimmy's mom, Elaine, was putting the final touches on a special dinner she'd spent all afternoon preparing. She walked into the hallway and called out to Jimmy, "Dinner's ready."

Dropping the towel from his hands, Jimmy dashed out of the bathroom door. Tearing down the steps, he reached the bottom in no time flat. His hand braced the banister. He swung his body in a half circle, landing firmly with both feet on the floor. He scurried into the kitchen.

Jimmy looked left toward the dinner table. The sight in front of him brought his feet to a screeching halt. Jimmy's dad, John, and his seven-year-old sister, Jillie, were sitting in their chairs around the table with giant smiles on their faces. In the middle of the dinner table was a big box with Jimmy's name on it. He knew it wasn't his birthday, and Christmas was almost two months away. Jimmy wondered what it could be.

The box was interesting, not because of its shape but because of the stripes on it.

Dad stood as if he were about to give a speech. "Jimmy," he began, "I brought this home from work today."

Jimmy's dad was a construction worker assigned to the crew rebuilding Yankee Stadium.

Jimmy didn't like the idea that the baseball stadium was going to be changed. Dad explained that the changes were for the better, and that Jimmy would love the new Yankee Stadium once it was completed in 1976.

Jimmy's mind was racing a mile a minute wondering what was in the pinstripe box. It was way too big for a hat or ball, and if it were a bat, it would be a much different shape. Jimmy couldn't stand the excitement any longer. He grabbed for the box and started to open it as fast as he could. Once the top was torn open, he peered down into the box and his mouth fell wide open. His dad helped him by slowly pulling the present out. Jillie was jumping out of her seat, sharing in the excitement.

"Relax, Jillie," said Mom. "You'll get to see it in just a second."

Jimmy lifted his gift straight up in the air and placed it on the floor next to him, while Dad pulled the box away.

"Wow! A stadium seat!" Jimmy exclaimed.

Dad proudly nodded his head. The seat looked old. It was made of wooden slabs, and its blue paint was faded and chipped. On the front of the seat was a brass plate about the shape and size of an egg. On the plate the number A1-33 was engraved.

Staring at the seat, Jimmy became more confused than ever.

"Let's eat dinner," said Dad, "and I'll tell you how I got this for you."

Mom dished out meat loaf, mashed potatoes, and peas. Jimmy didn't even notice the food on his plate, his eyes were glued to his father.

Dad began to tell the entire family how the crew spent the last three days tearing out all the old seats and throwing them away. All the seats were going to be taken apart, and the wooden slabs would be sold to baseball fans as memorabilia. Part of the Yankee Stadium renovation was replacing the wooden seats with new ones made out of plastic.

"Tell me about my seat," interrupted Jimmy.

"Hold on, the best is yet to come," stated Dad, and a hush fell over the dinner table as he continued. "To remove the seats, the bolts that secured them were loosened with electronic power wrenches. Every seat in the stadium was easily removed, with the exception of this one."

Jimmy's dad briefly pointed to seat A1-33.

"Where was this seat located?" asked Jimmy.

"Six rows behind the first base dugout," Dad responded. "For three days the crew tried to remove the seat. We broke wrenches, nothing we tried worked. Finally, Mr. Deavers, my foreman, announced that whoever removed the seat would receive a $50 bonus. Listen carefully, Jimmy. Here's the amazing part of the story. When it was my turn to try, I simply touched the seat and it lifted into my hands. I know this is crazy, but I could've sworn I heard a stadium crowd cheering like I was Mickey Mantle hitting home run number 500. When Mr. Deavers came over to give me the money, I wouldn't accept it. It just didn't seem right giving the seat to him, so I asked him if I could keep it and bring it home to you. He smiled and said, 'Sure, give it to the little ballplayer.' Jimmy, if this seat could talk, I bet it could tell some great Yankee stories."

CHAPTER 2

Throughout dinner, Jimmy was so excited about his gift he barely touched anything on his plate. Mom had to ask him three times if he wanted her homemade apple pie. Any other day the answer would have been yes, but not tonight.

"I'll take his," Jillie said with excitement.

"You know, Jillie, for a little girl, you sure can pack dessert away," said Dad.

Jillie gave a little giggle as she lifted the fork to her mouth.

Jimmy left the kitchen table and brought the stadium seat and the Yankee pinstripe box up to his room. Finding the right spot for each would take some time. Finally, the box was placed in his closet. Jimmy decided to keep his baseball glove, ball, and Yankee hat in the box. He also decided the box would be perfect for holding his collection of baseball trading cards. Deciding on a special location for the stadium seat would take a little bit more time.

Jimmy went from spot to spot until he decided exactly where he wanted it. Across from his bed was a window-ledge that overlooked the street. Jimmy and Jillie had spent many winter nights sitting at the window, watching the snowflakes pass through the glow of the streetlights. This would be the new home of Yankee Box Seat A1-33.

The only thing Jimmy had left to do that evening was call his two best friends. Ricky Birk and Mike Laffey had been Jimmy's Little League teammates for the past two years. The three friends did everything together, and Jimmy couldn't wait to share his exciting news. Jimmy quickly dialed Ricky's number. His first attempt was a disappointment. Mrs. Birk informed him that Ricky had homework to complete and wasn't allowed to talk on the phone until he was done. Jimmy hung up and dialed Mike's number. His buddy answered the phone on the first ring. After hearing about the stadium seat, Mike thought it would be fun to see it after school the next day. Jimmy, feeling proud, quickly agreed.

That night before he went to sleep, Jimmy stared at his seat for a long while. He wondered if the seat had feelings and missed not being at Yankee Stadium. Jimmy knew that the seat was just wood, paint, and steel. But somehow he knew why his father felt it wouldn't have been right to give the seat to Mr. Deavers for the $50 bonus. No matter how old it was, A1-33 should never be destroyed.

Jimmy got out of bed and walked over to the chair and sat in it for the first time. He pretended like he was watching a Yankees game from A1-33. Jimmy pretended he was eating a hotdog and trying to look over a woman with a tall hat so he could see the game better. Suddenly he thought he heard the sound of a crowd cheering. He jumped out of the chair and the room went silent. Jimmy shook his head in disbelief and decided he was more tired than he thought.

Through the darkness of the room, Jimmy continued to stare at his box seat. He couldn't keep his eyes off of it. The darkness soon became hazy and then slowly Jimmy was surrounded by light. Suddenly, Jimmy found himself walking out of the Yankee dugout. He turned and looked up into the seats. Standing in front of box seat A1-33 was an older man wearing a maroon blazer and blue pants. On his left hand was a furry glove. Jimmy knew he had seen this uniform before. The man was an usher at Yankee Stadium. Slowly he started walking toward Jimmy, and then he called his name.

"You've made two friends very happy," he said. "We know you can win it for us today."

The next thing Jimmy knew he was standing at home plate. On the mound, the pitcher was staring him down. There was a runner on first, and the scoreboard showed two outs. Before he stepped into the batter's box, Jimmy looked toward the outfield. Something about the stadium looked different, but he couldn't figure out what. And then Jimmy realized what was different. Instead of being on the center field warning track where they had always been, the famous monuments were now screened in behind it.

Jimmy heard the umpire call for him to step up to the plate, and he did. The first pitch was a fastball on the inside corner.

"Strike one," yelled the umpire.

Jimmy fouled the second pitch down the left field line for strike two. The next two throws missed the strike zone, bringing the count to two balls and two strikes.

Somehow, Jimmy knew the next pitch would be a waist-high fastball on the outside corner. He dug his spikes into the ground and re-gripped his bat. The pitch came in. Jimmy kept his eye on the ball and swung his bat even. Jimmy made solid contact, and the ball rocketed into deep center field. Jimmy started to run down the first base line. Everyone in the stadium could see the center fielder angling back toward the ball as he was getting closer to the fence. The outfielder's glove went up as he leaped toward it.

"Jimmy! Jimmy, wake up," his mom called, "come down for break-fast and hurry or you're going to be late for school."

Jimmy opened his eyes. He was in bed. He had fallen asleep. What a dream, he thought to himself.

CHAPTER 3

Jimmy daydreamed about baseball during his entire walk to school. He imagined he had blasted a last inning home run and had won the World Series for the Yanks. News reporters and the crowd of fans were trying to get his attention. He thought how exciting it would feel to be a hometown hero, especially in front of all his friends.

"Hey, Jimmy, wait up," yelled Ricky Birk.

Jimmy snapped back to reality as his buddy came running up the street from behind him. "Ricky, I tried to call you last night," said Jimmy.

"Yeah, I know. My mother wouldn't let me do anything but home-work. Why'd you call?" asked Ricky.

"I got this great present from my dad's work yesterday."

"What, a bucket of nails?" sneered Ricky.

"No, listen up and I'll tell you."

By the time Jimmy had finished the story about the stadium seat, the two boys were standing in front of their school, P.S. 5.

"How about coming over to my house today with Mike?" Jimmy asked.

"Um, all right. I'll meet you at the bicycle rack at three o'clock," responded Ricky.

Jimmy waved goodbye and then walked in the direction of his class-room. As he continued through the school corridor, he was bothered by Ricky's reaction toward the stadium seat. Why wasn't he excited? Jimmy wondered. Regardless of whether anyone else thought his dad's gift was special, Jimmy knew A1-33 was something really great.

Concentrating in class was difficult for Jimmy that day. His mind kept drifting back to parts of the previous night's dream. The Yankee memorials were enclosed behind the center field fence rather than be-ing on the warning track where he had always seen them. Jimmy wondered if the ball he hit was caught. Why did Mom have to wake me up at exactly that moment? The three o'clock bell rang and Jimmy rushed out of class to meet his friends.

Ricky and Mike were waiting at the bicycle rack as planned.

"Let's go to your house and have a seat," yelled Mike.

"Yeah, are we going to play musical chairs?" asked Ricky.

Both of Jimmy's friends started to laugh.

"If you guys realized what a great ballpark Yankee Stadium is, you'd know that having a stadium seat is a great present," said Jimmy defensively.

Mike put his hand on Jimmy's shoulder, "Relax, McNeil. We're just playing with you."

Jimmy gave his friends a half-smile and said, "Come on, I'll race both of you to my house."

The three boys ran all the way. Mike and Jimmy were usually the same speed, and Ricky always ran the fastest, but not this day. Jimmy led the pack and made it to his front door well in front of his friends. As he grabbed the doorknob, he knew why he had won the race, not because he was the fastest, but because today he wanted it more. His dad had always taught him that in anything you try, you may find others that have more experience, better skills, or more ability. But those who become the best are those who want to succeed the most.

Ricky and Mike entered the house ten steps behind Jimmy. The sweet smell of Jimmy's Mom's chocolate cake filled the air. Ricky and Mike went right into the kitchen. Jimmy rushed upstairs to see A1-33. As he entered the room, much to his surprise, he found his stadium seat turned around. The chair's back was facing him and the front was directed toward the window. Jimmy figured his mom must have been cleaning the room and turned it around accidentally. He smiled at A1-33, and then headed back downstairs to join his friends for cake and milk.

"Where'd you go, Jimmy?" asked Ricky.

"Just upstairs. Why?" Jimmy returned.

"We thought you were going to bring down your seat," Mike said.

"No, you'll have to go upstairs if you want to see it," said Jimmy.

Mom smiled to herself as she left the boys alone in the kitchen. They quickly finished their snack and then cleared the table.

The boys climbed up the stairs, taking two steps at a time. Within seconds they were standing inside Jimmy's bedroom. Jimmy's eyes grew wide with shock. A1-33 was now turned back around to its original position! Jimmy tried to remember if he had turned the seat back around. I must have, he thought. Mike asked if he could sit in the seat.

"Not now, I don't want you to break it," said Jimmy.

"It's a seat. You're supposed to sit in it," Ricky said.

"I know, but it's not braced to the floor," Jimmy explained.

It seemed clear by the look on his friends' faces, that Mike and Ricky thought Jimmy was taking his present a bit too seriously.

As the afternoon continued, the three teammates talked about Little League. They discussed games from the previous year, and wondered how the team would do this season. The conversation soon shifted to great Yankee games they'd watched and how many autographs they had for their baseball card collections. Mike told Jimmy and Ricky that he was going to save his baseball cards forever and that maybe some day they would be worth a lot of money. The afternoon went by quickly. Mike and Ricky headed home around suppertime.

During dinner, Mom asked Jimmy if his friends enjoyed seeing the Yankee seat.

"I think they did," said Jimmy. "But they don't think it's as big a deal as I do."

"You know, Jimmy, what's important to you may not be as important to everyone else," Mom said. "You need to learn to accept this in your friends."

Jimmy nodded his head and finished the spaghetti on his plate.

Later that evening, when Jimmy went to sleep, he kept thinking about Mom's comments.

"I know that A1-33 is part of baseball's great history, and of all the kids who love baseball, I am the luckiest," Jimmy said softly to himself.

As he closed his eyes and began to fall asleep, he faintly heard a voice say, "Thank you, Jimmy."

CHAPTER 4

Jimmy's eyes opened wide. He jumped out of bed and ran to the window. With both hands bracing the arms of the stadium seat, Jimmy peered out to see if it had snowed overnight. A wonderful feeling came over him as the street revealed a light, fluffy blanket over it. There was something special about a Christmas morning with fresh fallen snow. Looking at the clock, he discovered it was only six a.m. He knew that it was way too early to wake up his parents.

Jimmy heard the door of his room creak open and saw Jillie sneak inside.

"Jimmy, let's wake up Mom and Dad."

"No, we have to wait until seven o'clock. You know the rules," said Jimmy.

They both spent the next hour trying to guess what holiday surprises were downstairs waiting for them. Jimmy didn't know what to expect this year. He felt he was too old for toys, yet he still loved to play games.

When the clock finally struck seven, Jimmy and Jillie rushed into their parents' room. Jillie leaped on top of the bed waking up Mom and Dad.

"Let's go. It's Christmas morning!" she exclaimed.

Mom and Dad slowly lifted their heads off of their pillows. Soon the entire family walked down the stairs. As they turned toward the living room, Jillie gasped with excitement. The Christmas tree was shining brightly, creating a beautiful reflection off the sea of gifts. The McNeils all scrambled to find boxes with their names on them. Jimmy knew each year his gifts were always great. This year he received winter clothes, two box games, and a book about Cooperstown and the Baseball Hall of Fame.

Over in the corner, Jimmy examined a gift with his name on it. He maneuvered his way through the paper and presents to reach it. Everyone became quiet as Jimmy picked up his gift and held it in his hands. On top of the present was a card that read, "Jimmy, I hope you enjoy this gift. It is a special gift for you." Jimmy looked up at his mom and dad with a smile.

"It came in the mail two days ago," Mom said. "We don't know who it's from."

"Open it up and let's see what's in the mystery box," Dad said.

Jimmy immediately followed his father's direction and unwrapped the gift. When he was finished, his face lit up as bright as the Christmas tree. It was the most beautiful piece of leather Jimmy had ever seen. He lifted the baseball glove out of the box and slid it onto his hand. His dad got off the couch and walked over to Jimmy, his eyes never leaving the baseball glove. "It sure is great looking, son," Dad said. "Is there a note inside the box saying who it's from?"

"No, just the glove," said Jimmy as he began pounding it with his right fist in an attempt to break in the new leather.

With a confused look on his face, Dad picked up the card that was on the box and read it to himself. He then turned to his wife and shrugged his shoulders. Mom walked toward him, and together they entered the kitchen reading the card, talking low so they couldn't be heard. Jimmy focused on the glove. It was the best he had ever seen. But even through all the excitement, Jimmy couldn't help but wonder who had sent it.

It was a great Christmas day. Jimmy played with his sister all afternoon until it was time to go to their grandparents' house for the traditional holiday gathering. They didn't return home until almost midnight.

Jimmy entered his room and went over to his glove, which he had placed on A1-33 earlier. He put the glove on his hand and tried to close it as if he were catching a ball. The glove didn't move much. Jimmy knew it needed a lot of work before he could use it effectively in the spring. He returned the glove to the stadium seat where it was put away for the evening. Shortly thereafter he went to bed, and in no time at all, fell asleep.

Throughout the night, Jimmy tossed and turned in his bed. His sleep was interrupted by a recurring dream. In his dream, Jimmy continually oiled his glove and placed a baseball strategically in the glove's palm. He would then bend the fingers inward so the glove almost resembled the shape of a shovel. Jimmy then took a piece of string and wrapped it around the glove, closed it on the ball, and tied the string tight. During the course of the dream, Jimmy heard a voice repeatedly saying, "Every good infielder shapes his glove in the form of a scoop, it helps you dig out low ground balls."

The very next day upon waking, Jimmy ran to his father's workshop in the basement of the house. He searched through every tool drawer until he found the perfect cord of twine. Then, in the same method he had dreamt about the previous night, he tied a ball up inside his glove. Jimmy made sure his glove formed the shape of a scoop. When it was completed to his satisfaction, he decided to leave it tied for a whole month.

CHAPTER 5

It was late March and Little League practice was just beginning. As Jimmy was getting dressed, the feeling of excitement made him so anxious he had a difficult time pulling his jeans over his feet. Once his pants were on, Jimmy tore through his dresser drawers and pulled out his baseball T-shirt. Jimmy knew the weather outside was still chilly and that it would be best to dress warm. He grabbed his gray sweatshirt from the closet.

Jimmy felt this would be the best first practice of any season he had ever had. Jimmy had just turned twelve-years-old, and was now a senior member of his Little League team. This would be his third straight year playing for the Blue Sox. Jimmy's team manager for the previous two years had been Mr. Whitehill, and he would be back again this year as well. Jimmy, Mike, and Ricky thought Mr. Whitehill was the best manager in the league. Mr. Whitehill worked the team hard and taught them a lot about baseball strategy.

Finally dressed, Jimmy walked over to A1-33. He reached out and grabbed his glove from the seat. Jimmy slid it over his hand and pounded it a few times: a routine he had repeated throughout the long New York winter. Looking at A1-33, Jimmy smiled and thought, baseball is finally here!

"Jimmy. Jimmy," Mom called. "Breakfast is ready."

"Coming," hollered Jimmy as he rushed down the stairs and into the kitchen, joining Dad at the breakfast table.

"Whoa," said Dad, "slow down and save some of that energy for today's practice."

"Don't worry, I have plenty of energy," said Jimmy.

Mom carried Jimmy's breakfast over to the table. As she placed it in front of him, Jimmy looked up at her and smiled. It was egg-dipped bread, a cross between scrambled eggs and French toast. It was his favorite breakfast. Mom called this, "Eggbread, breakfast for a hometown champion." She watched as Jimmy dove right into his plate.

As Jimmy continued to eat, Jillie walked into the kitchen from the den and plopped herself down in a chair next to her brother. She placed both elbows on the table in front of her and used the palms of her hands as a chin rest. Without saying a word, she just stared at Jimmy.

"What are you doing? You're giving me the willies," said Jimmy.

"I'm just waiting for you to finish breakfast so we can watch Saturday morning cartoons together."

"I can't. I have my first Little League practice today."

"So what," replied Jillie.

"Jillie, any other day Jimmy would watch TV with you," said Dad. "But practice is very important to a ballplayer."

With a dissatisfied look, Jillie sulked away from the breakfast table and into the den.

"Practice is important, but remember you only have one sister," said Dad after Jillie had left. "Make sure you spend time with her too."

Jimmy looked at his father and he nodded his head in agreement.

"OK Dad," said Jimmy.

"What time is practice, son?" asked Dad.

"Ten o'clock," Jimmy answered.

"Do you need a ride to the ballpark?"

"Nope. I'm going to walk with Ricky and Mike."

"Well then you better get going. It's 9:45."

Jimmy quickly put down his fork, grabbed his glove and waved good-bye to his family as he flew out of the front door.

Ricky and Mike were both waiting outside their houses with their baseball gloves in hand. The three teammates rushed all the way to Welty Park. At exactly ten o'clock they entered through the gated door on the third baseline. Jimmy breathed a sigh of relief knowing they weren't late for practice on the first day.

Walking onto the infield, Jimmy immediately noticed the ground was hard and hadn't yet thawed from winter. During the spring and summer, the infield dirt at Welty Park was almost like powder.

Across the infield, Mr. Whitehill was waving the boys over to the first base dugout. They quickly trotted over and joined the rest of the team. Jimmy noticed some new players and realized they were mostly ten-year-olds who were playing their first year in the Major Little League.

"Everyone on the bench!" Mr. Whitehill called out.

Everyone scurried over and grabbed a seat as they were directed. The team stared attentively at their manager, waiting to hear what he had to say.

Mr. Whitehill introduced himself and his assistant coach, Mr. Roshay, to the entire team. He then asked all the ballplayers to state their name and age, so that the new players could become familiar with their teammates.

"It's important to pay attention in practice," said Mr. Whitehill. "This is the way we prepare for the season."

"Practice hard and play hard," added Mr. Roshay.

Mr. Whitehill then told his players everyone needed to respect and encourage each other, and that each person was an important part of the team.

As Mr. Whitehill was finishing his first pep talk of the season, Jimmy's eyes moved toward Mr. Roshay who was in the process of grabbing a brown canvas bat bag. He loosened the rope tie at the top and began taking the equipment out. There were seven bats ranging in size from twenty-seven to thirty-two inches long. He placed these against the fence with the handles up. There were a bunch of used baseballs and four red Little League helmets with ear protection on both sides.

"Grab a ball and pair up," Mr. Whitehill told his players. "I want everyone to loosen up. Remember to go nice and easy, this is your first day out."

"McNeil, do you want to toss the ball with me?" Jimmy turned around. Standing there with a ball in his hand was Joey Petruto. Joey was also twelve-years-old and had played with Jimmy for the previous two years as well. Jimmy thought Joey was the best third baseman in the league. He was a little shorter and stockier than Jimmy. He had quick hands, and it was rare that a ball could get by him down the third base line.

"Yes!" Jimmy answered with a smile.

Both boys ran onto the field and threw easy, just as Mr. Whitehill had instructed.

"Great glove!" Joey yelled to Jimmy as they were throwing. "Where'd you get it?"

"A Christmas present," Jimmy answered, as he released the ball from his hand.

Joey nodded his head with approval as he extended his arm out to catch Jimmy's toss. This was the first time Jimmy had a chance to use his glove. It felt good, but not completely broken in.

While the team loosened up, Mr. Whitehill and Mr. Roshay continuously walked by the ballplayers, watching them and talking only to themselves. After fifteen minutes, Mr. Whitehill called for a fielding drill. He began by assigning positions. "Joey Petruto, third base. Ricky Birk, shortstop. Jimmy McNeil, go ahead and take second. And David Rockman, you take the bag at first."

Jimmy felt proud to be called out for the first drill. He knew Mr. Whitehill was placing the ballplayers in the positions where he felt they belonged. Jimmy loved playing second base, but last year his playing time had been mostly in right field. There were older and better players who played the second base position.

Mr. Whitehill flipped the ball to the star lefty pitcher, Bobby Sharples. He then asked Mike Laffey, who was the team's first string catcher, to warm Bobby up along the first base line.

"No fastballs today, Bobby!" Mr. Whitehill said with a concerned voice. "It's cold and you need to protect your arm."

Bobby and Mike ran together down the first base line until they were in the foul territory of the outfield. Mike paced out forty-six feet, the distance in Little League from the pitching rubber to home plate. Mike then crouched down in a catcher's position and began warming Bobby up.

Eleven-year-old Stanley Johnson was asked to stay at home plate, and catch balls for Mr. Whitehill during the infield drill. The remainder of the team followed Mr. Roshay to the outfield for their practice.

"Okay, first base," yelled Mr. Whitehill, indicating where the infielder should throw the ball.

Mr. Whitehill hit a chopper to Joey at third, who fielded it cleanly and threw to David at first. Continuing in rotation, Mr. Whitehill hit a ground ball to shortstop. Ricky made a nice play and fired the ball to first. It was now Jimmy's turn. As he was waiting for the ball to be hit, he began to get a nervous feeling in his stomach.

Mr. Whitehill flipped the ball in the air, swung his bat, and sent the ball bouncing toward Jimmy. Jimmy stood still, as if he was frozen in place. The ball approached him, he reached out to field the ball, and suddenly it bounced up and over his right shoulder. Jimmy turned his head around and watched the ball roll out to right field.

"Come on, Jimmy, take another one!" yelled Mr. Whitehill.

Jimmy positioned himself again. This time the ball seemed to hug the ground. Jimmy slowly approached it, extending his glove outward, but not in time. The ball went under his glove and through his legs. Jimmy hung his head toward the ground in disappointment.

"Go out and get the balls, Jimmy," Mr. Whitehill directed.

Jimmy did as his manager asked. As he ran out to get them, he heard Mr. Whitehill call to David Rockman, "This one's coming to you!"

Mr. Whitehill continued to hit balls around the infield. Jimmy couldn't help but feel embarrassed. I wish I could crawl into a hole, he thought to himself.

While Jimmy continued to wait for his next chance, he looked toward the first base line. Standing at the fence, he noticed a man with gray hair. The man was wearing an old-fashioned style Yankee hat and a faded blue winter jacket. He was wearing gloves and rubbing his hands together. He stared straight at Jimmy. Jimmy stared back and thought the man seemed familiar, although he didn't know how.

"Jimmy, come on, pay attention! Practice is on the field," hollered Mr. Whitehill.

Jimmy snapped-to and prepared for his next try. The ball came off the bat in even hops, directly to him. Jimmy felt the ball land in his glove, and he squeezed it with all of his might. He then threw wide of David Rockman at first base. The ball rolled back to the fence.

"Better," said Mr. Whitehill.

"Better, but still awful," Jimmy mumbled to himself.

He looked back toward the first base stands. The man he was expecting to see was gone.

Practice lasted for about another hour. Each player only took five swings at bat since the weather was cold. Jimmy made contact with the ball only once, which was a foul pop up. David Rockman was the only one who pounded the ball, but that was no surprise to anyone. David was the best hitter on the team. He was a great athlete and had made last year's Little League All-Star team.

After batting practice, Mr. Whitehill called the team back to the dugout.

"This was a good first day," he said. "Opening game is on April 11th, and we'll need a lot more practices before we're ready. I'll see everyone at two o'clock tomorrow."

On the way home, Mike and Ricky talked about how great the practice was. Jimmy hardly spoke. This was not the best day he had ever had. He was cold and upset at the way he had played. Jimmy just wanted to get home.

CHAPTER 6

After dinner, Jimmy took his glove and ball and walked downstairs to the basement, which was dark and cold. The flooring was gray concrete, and the walls were made of cinder blocks. Jimmy's parents never objected to him throwing a ball in the basement because nothing could be damaged. Sitting on the floor with his back against the wall, Jimmy repeatedly tossed the ball against the opposite wall and then caught it, as it ricocheted back in even bounces. Why couldn't I catch the ball this easy during practice, he thought.

Suddenly Jimmy found himself sitting in Yankee Stadium, six rows behind the Yankee dugout. The stands were almost empty. There were a few people scattered around, and a maintenance crew was cleaning the stadium. On the field, the Yankees were taking practice. The ballplayers were not in full uniform. They wore baseball pants and white undershirts with long blue sleeves. In the outfield were four players running from right field to left field. Jimmy knew they were loosening up. Two ground crew members dashed out to the mound and removed a screen that protected the pitcher during batting practice.

To Jimmy's shock, Yogi Berra came out of the dugout. Jimmy started looking around the stadium almost in panic. He became confused. Yogi Berra? What is this, an old timer's game? He wondered.

"Sit back, Jimmy, and just watch," said a calm voice.

"Who said that?" Jimmy asked, but no one answered.

Jimmy squirmed uncomfortably in his seat. His eyes wandered across the field. Yogi Berra was holding a long, thin bat called a fungo bat, as he walked toward home plate. Charging out of the dugout came five ballplayers. Jimmy now sat still. The tall catcher standing next to Yogi at home plate was none other than Elston Howard. Jimmy quickly looked around the rest of the infield. At third base was Clete Boyer, and the shortstop was Tony Kubeck. At second base was Bobby Richardson, and first base was Joe Pepitone.

Where am I? This Yankee team hasn't played for years, he thought.

Again, the voice that seemed to come from behind him whispered calmly, "Watch, Jimmy, and learn."

Yogi Berra began hitting balls to his Yankee infield. Jimmy paid particular attention to Bobby Richardson. He made every play look easy.

"Keep watching him, Jimmy. See how he moves toward the ball?

He charges the ball so he can control it, bending over to play it better. When he approaches the ball, his eyes never leave it. He lowers his glove toward the dirt and scoops grounders right up," said the voice.

The next ball Yogi Berra sent toward second base was hit hard. Bobby Richardson charged the ball. It took a bad hop, bounced over his glove, hit him square in the chest, and finally landed in front of him. The Yankee second baseman picked up the ball, whipped it to first, and hustled back to position.

"Richardson is one of the best second baseman I've seen play at this ballpark," whispered the voice.

Jimmy was beginning to recognize the voice.

Jimmy looked down at his glove. He felt uneasy and confused as he picked himself up off the basement floor.

"I must have fallen asleep," he said to himself.

With a perplexed look on his face, Jimmy made his way upstairs to his bedroom. He flipped his glove and ball onto A1-33. He couldn't stop thinking about what a great second baseman Bobby Richardson was as he climbed into bed.

CHAPTER 7

The next morning, Jimmy did chores around the house to help out his parents. His big assignment was to clean out the garage. Jimmy's Little League practice began at two o'clock, so he was moving as fast as he could. While he was working, every thought he had was about his previous night's dream. He was thinking about it so much, before he knew it, he had finished cleaning the garage.

Jimmy ran into the house to tell his father he was done. After a detailed inspection from Dad, Jimmy got the thumbs up for a job well done.

"When are you leaving for practice?" Dad asked.

"Right now," replied Jimmy enthusiastically.

Collecting his glove, Jimmy traveled to the field by himself. It was only 12:30, but he wanted to get there early.

It was a great day outside. The sun was shining, and the temperature was slightly warmer than the day before. Jimmy arrived at Welty Park with plenty of time to spare. He grabbed a seat in the stands on the first base line and stared out at the field. While day dreaming, Jimmy thought about Bobby Richardson attacking the baseball after it was hit to him during the Yankee infield drill.

"Hello, Jimmy. You're here pretty early," hollered Mr. Whitehill.

Jimmy was startled by his voice.

"I know, Mr. Whitehill. Guess I'm just anxious to play," Jimmy hollered back.

Mr. Whitehill turned away with a smile and headed to the dugout. Like every manager and coach, Mr. Whitehill appreciated an athlete who looked forward to playing.

By two o'clock, the entire team had arrived. Mr. Whitehill had everyone loosen up by throwing nice and easy, just as he had instructed the previous day.

"I'll call the infielders, everyone else will go to the outfield with Mr. Roshay," directed Mr. Whitehill. "I'd like Joey at third, Ricky at shortstop, Jimmy and Stanley Johnson at second, and David Rockman at first base."

Jimmy's heart dropped to his stomach. He immediately knew Mr. Whitehall had assigned both he and Stanley to second base because he wanted to see someone else play the position. Knowing his previous day's performance wasn't impressive, Jimmy quickly became determined to show his manager that he was the best player for the job. He began by running out to second base and preparing himself for the toughest play possible. Stanley followed and stood behind Jimmy while they waited for instructions.

Mr. Whitehill began in the usual fashion by hitting the ball in rotation beginning with third base. When it became the second baseman's turn, he yelled out, "Jimmy your ball first."

Stanley stepped further back, allowing Jimmy more room. Jimmy wanted this ball, and a look of total concentration came over him.

The ball cracked off the bat. It was a hard hit grounder. Jimmy's instincts took over, and he bent forward while charging the ball. Jimmy extended his glove and made a beautiful scoop. He threw the ball perfectly to David Rockman at first, and hustled behind Stanley, who took a step up and waited for his turn. Mr. Whitehill hit a grounder to Stanley who quickly made his way to the ball. It bounced up in his glove and he bobbled it slightly before taking full control. Once it was in hand, Stanley threw the ball cleanly to David at first.

Within a minute, the rotation came back around to Jimmy. Again, Mr. Whitehill hit a hard grounder. Jimmy came charging in, keeping his eye on the ball. The infield, still hard from winter, caused the ball to take a bad hop. It came up on Jimmy, who was in front of the ball, hitting him squarely in the chest. The ball landed directly on the ground in front of him. Jimmy quickly picked up the ball and threw it sharply to first base.

"Great play!" exclaimed Mr. Whitehill, who then walked onto the field, halfway between home plate and the pitcher's mound.

The entire infield became quiet as Mr. Whitehill said, "Jimmy just made a textbook play on a ball that was hard to control. He stayed in front of it the entire time and played it with his body."

"The way you played that bad hop reminded me of Bobby Richardson," Mr. Whitehill said, turning toward Jimmy.

Jimmy felt good about his play, but Mr. Whitehill's reference to Bobby Richardson stunned him. What a coincidence, Jimmy thought. Jimmy took it as a great compliment and hustled back to the second base position to continue practice.

Throughout practice, Jimmy continued to field the ball well. During batting practice, he failed to hit the ball like he had hoped. Overall, though, he felt more confident than he had the day before.

At four o'clock, Mr. Whitehill called the team in for their daily pep talk and then ended practice. Jimmy walked home with Mike and Ricky. They passed Mike's house first, and Ricky and Jimmy continued on.

"Ricky, do you ever remember your dreams when you wake up in the morning?" asked Jimmy.

"Yeah. I must dream about food a lot, because I always wake up hungry," said Ricky.

The boys both laughed, and then talked all the way to Ricky's house.

"See you tomorrow in school," Ricky said as he walked up to his front door.

For the remainder of the walk home, Jimmy thought about Mr. Whitehill's comparison to Bobby Richardson. It made Jimmy think about some of the dreams he had had over the last five months. The first baseball dream had occurred the night he received the stadium seat from his dad. At Christmas, he had dreamt about how he should take care of his new glove, which he did all winter long. And last night, he dreamt about watching a Yankee practice with players who were active when he was only a year old! Jimmy felt goose bumps run up and down his spine, and his walk soon turned to a run. Jimmy was anxious to talk to his parents.

Jimmy entered the house and found his dad watching a basketball game on TV.

"Hi, Dad. What are you doing?" asked Jimmy.

"The Knicks are playing the Celtics. Want to watch the game with me?" Dad asked back.

Staring at his father, Jimmy asked if they could talk for a few minutes. Seeing a worried look on Jimmy's face, Dad turned off the TV and swung around in his chair.

"What's bothering you?" Dad asked concerned. "Was practice okay, today?"

"Yeah, practice was great. I did a lot better than yesterday," said Jimmy.

"Well, what'd you want to talk about?" Dad said with a smile.

"Do you remember the day you brought A1-33 home from Yankee Stadium?"

"Of course."

"Don't you think it's strange that no one was able to remove the stadium seat, not even with tools. But when you tried, the seat just lifted into your hands?"

"I never thought about it. The bolts were probably loosened by one of the other guys, and it just gave in on my turn."

"I don't know, a lot of weird things have happened since we got the seat."

Looking confused, Dad asked, "Weird things? What are you talking about?"

"Well, how about the glove I received as a Christmas present? No one knows where it came from," said Jimmy. "How do you explain that?"

"I would have to guess that it was sent by either Aunt Alice or your grandfather," said Dad. "Whoever gave it to you probably thought it would be more fun to make us all wonder about it. Now come on, I've explained how we got the seat, and who probably sent you the baseball glove. So what's this really about?"

Jimmy proceeded to tell his father about the dream he had the first night A1-33 was brought home. Jimmy's father was now tilting his head toward his son, listening intently.

Jimmy continued, "I even remember the conversation I had with the man."

Then Jimmy stopped talking. A look of discovery fell over his face. The man he had dreamt about in the usher's uniform was the same man he had seen watching his Little League practice!

"What man did you talk with?" Dad asked.

"Never mind. Let's forget the whole conversation," Jimmy said as he turned around and slowly walked out of the room.

Entering his bedroom, Jimmy dropped down and sat on the floor with his back against the bed, facing A1-33. He couldn't stop thinking about the image of the man. Jimmy sat for the longest time staring at A1-33. He stared at it like he was waiting for something to happen. But nothing did. Finally, Jimmy stood up and walked downstairs to watch the game with his father.

CHAPTER 8

It was spring recess and Jimmy had planned to practice baseball all week. Mr. Whitehill had scheduled four drills. In addition, Jimmy and the guys planned to take batting practice on their own. They were determined to be ready for opening day on April 11th.

On Tuesday morning, Jimmy' father tiptoed his way into his son's bedroom.

"Wake up, Jimmy," he said softly. "We're going to be late for work."

Looking up at his dad still half-asleep, Jimmy was wondering what he meant.

"We're going to be late for work," Dad repeated.

Jimmy propped himself up in bed.

"Dad, what are you talking about?" Jimmy asked.

"I thought you might enjoy coming with me to the construction site," said Dad.

"Construction site? You mean Yankee Stadium?" asked Jimmy excitedly.

"That's exactly what I mean. Now get dressed and we'll stop for breakfast along the way."

As Jimmy was jumping out of bed, his dad reminded him to wear his Yankee hat. Jimmy hustled to get ready. He couldn't wait to get to the stadium.

When they arrived at the stadium, Jimmy and his father entered through a fenced door at the back of the ballpark. Positioned by the gate was a security guard. Recognizing John McNeil, he smiled and waved them through. Once inside the fenced-in area, Jimmy looked up to see a sign over a big double door. The sign read: "Players' Entrance."

Jimmy's eyes almost popped out of his head. He'd been to Yankee Stadium many times, but it had always been through the fan gates. He felt important walking through this gate. As he made his way through the players' entrance, Jimmy couldn't help but imagine he was a major leaguer going to the stadium for a game.

Jimmy stopped to look at the massive pillars that support the stadium stands. Straight-ahead was the opening passage to the field box seats. Jimmy was expecting to see home plate and a well-groomed infield. But what he saw instead was something much different.

The field did not look like a field at all. The field looked like a construction site. There were cranes and bulldozers. Scraps of iron were scattered everywhere. Workbenches with all sorts of tools were placed all over. A construction crew wearing work shirts and protective hard hats had replaced ballplayers in pinstriped uniforms and baseball hats.

Jimmy's dad gave his son instructions for the day, which included safety precautions.

While Jimmy sat on an iron girder watching all the activity around him, his mind floated back to his dream of Bobby Richardson at Yankee practice.

Jimmy looked over to the right, where first base was to be located. There were three men standing over a workbench having an argument. One of the men was dressed in workman's clothes while the other two were wearing business jackets and ties. All three had hard hats on. They were looking at a blueprint that was rolled out on the worktable. Their tone of voice was loud, and it was easy to hear what they were saying.

The man on the left was saying that he represented the Baseball Commissioner's office. He rudely told the two other men that the Yankee monuments could not stay on the playing field any longer.

Jimmy quickly looked toward the section of the stadium he recognized as straightaway center field. There they were, the three famous Yankee monuments. Each stood about five feet high and three feet wide. They were made of stone and all had engraved images of the individuals they represented: Miller Huggins, Lou Gehrig, and Babe Ruth.

Jimmy's head snapped back toward the workbench when he heard one of the men raise his voice.

"These monuments have been part of Yankee Stadium for as long as I can remember," he said passionately. "They mean a lot to the players and the fans. The monuments stay, and that's the position of the New York Yankee Management."

"You have no choice," interrupted the man from the commissioner's office. "This field won't be approved for major league play unless those monuments are removed from the playing field."

The construction crew came to a complete silence as everyone listened intently. Mr. Deavers, the foreman, was the third man at the blueprint table. He threw his hands up in the air and spoke in an impatient manner.

"Look, I have a crane here and you both are costing this project a lot of money. Now do I remove the monuments or leave them alone?"

While the argument was going on, Jimmy had made his way to the blueprint table.

"Why can't you build the center field fence in front of the monuments so they won't be in the way of play but still be seen by the fans?" asked Jimmy looking up toward the three men who were still arguing.

The representative from the Commissioner's office looked toward Mr. Deavers.

"Who is this kid?" he asked.

Before he could answer, the man from the Yankee office smiled. He turned to the others.

"What a great idea," he said. " It's 461 feet from home plate to straightaway center. It's the biggest outfield in the major leagues. We can reconstruct and design the fence so the field is a little shorter, and leave the monuments visible as the kid said. Everyone will be happy!"

At this point, Jimmy's dad came rushing over to pull Jimmy away from the table. By the look on Dad's face, Jimmy thought he was in big trouble.

"What's your name, son?" asked the man from the Yankees.

"Jimmy McNeil."

"He's Mac's son," added Mr. Deavers.

"Well kid," continued the man from Yankees management. "You just saved the Yankee monuments. I owe you one."

Jimmy looked up and grinned. The silence of the stadium soon began to disappear, and the noise of the construction site resumed. Jimmy felt his father's hand on his shoulder guiding him toward the first base dugout.

When they reached the dugout, Jimmy's dad told his son, "I'm not sure whether to reward you or punish you. I know you're just trying to help, but you have to mind your own business around here."

There was a moment of silence, and then Dad looked at Jimmy in an approving manner. "You did great, son. Now come this way, there's someone I want you to meet."

They began walking up the stands behind the first base dugout. All of the stadium seats were gone. Trying to calculate where A1-33 would have been, Jimmy's eyes progressively moved upward one row at a time. Lifting his head at row six, Jimmy expected to see the empty spot, which would have been the previous home of his stadium seat.

But to Jimmy's surprise, he did not see an empty area. Instead, sitting on the concrete where A1-33 would have been positioned, was the man Jimmy had seen the previous week at his Little League practice.

Jimmy's dad turned to him and said, "I'd like you to meet Sam, a Yankee usher for over fifty years."

Jimmy felt a weird sensation run through him. His mouth was locked shut from the surprise, and he could hardly speak a word.

His dad continued, "When the stadium closed last year, Sam retired. He's the greatest Yankee fan of all time, and I bet he could tell you some great stories from the old days."

Sam looked down at Jimmy, winked, and began to speak.

"Go back to work Mac," Sam said. "I'll sit and talk with Jimmy for awhile."

Jimmy's dad smiled at both Sam and Jimmy as he turned and walked away.

A warm smile grew upon Sam's face. This made Jimmy feel at ease.

"That was a very special thing you just did, Jimmy," said Sam. "You saved the Yankee monuments."

"It wasn't me, who saved the Yankee monuments, was it?" asked Jimmy.

Sam patted his hand on the concrete as a gesture for Jimmy to sit down next to him.

"Let me tell you a Yankee story no one has ever heard before," Sam said. "When this stadium first opened up, I was assigned to this very section. I took care of each and every seat as if it was my very own. I loved the fans, the games, and the New York Yankees. Not because they were the hometown team, but because they offered the game of baseball a sense of joy, honor, and respect."

Sam paused for a second before continuing.

"The great athletes who played on this field will be talked about like the Greek Olympiads. More importantly, Jimmy, the Yankees and this stadium brought people together for a common goal. During hard times like the Depression and World War II, fans of the Yanks came to this ballpark. The fans found happiness, comfort and a sense of security. It seemed almost magical. Right here where I'm sitting was the location of something that was the most special of all. This is where Mrs. Gehrig sat and watched her husband play in Yankee pinstripes."

"*The* Lou Gehrig," interrupted Jimmy excitedly.

"That's right," continued Sam. "Now, as you know, Lou Gehrig became ill, which forced him to retire from baseball well before his time. No one loved the game of baseball more than he did, that is with the exception of one person—his wife. Mrs. Gehrig loved her husband so much she was thankful to the game for the happiness it brought him. Mrs. Gehrig's devotion and commitment to her husband created a positive energy surrounding this entire section, but most importantly, to Box Seat A1-33."

Jimmy felt a sensation run throughout his entire body when Sam mentioned his box seat. He gave Sam his complete attention.

"During Lou's farewell speech, Mrs. Gehrig asked one request of me. That her stadium seat be saved only for those who truly loved the game of baseball. On January 31, 1963, I had a dream that Yankee Stadium was being torn apart and all the seats were being destroyed. Through the construction dust, I saw A1-33 shining a light from its brass numerical plate. Standing next to the seat, I saw a boy in a Yankee hat. Last fall when all the seats were being removed, I watched A1-33 refuse to be destroyed. Then, as your dad lifted the seat up into his hands and carried it out of the stadium, I knew right away it was going home to the Yankee fan I had dreamt about almost eleven years earlier."

"You mean . . ." Jimmy stammered.

"Jimmy, that boy in the Yankee hat was you," said Sam.

A chill shot up Jimmy's back. In a crackling voice Jimmy said, "My birthday is January 31, 1963."

Sam smiled and tapped the beak of Jimmy's Yankee hat.

"I know," said Sam. "Cherish A1-33, Jimmy, and it will cherish you."

"I will. I promise," said Jimmy.

"You know, I won't be able to watch a game at this ballpark until 1976 when the renovation is completed. Would you mind if I watch your Little League games instead?" asked Sam.

"I wouldn't mind at all!"

Sam turned and walked away. Jimmy wanted to stop him. There were so many questions he needed to ask, but didn't have time to. Jimmy didn't get too disappointed, though. He knew he was going to see Sam again.

CHAPTER 9

You always get a special kick on opening day,
no matter how many you go through. You look forward
to it like a birthday party when you're a kid.
You think something wonderful is going to happen.

–Joe DiMaggio

Opening day was always exciting. It seemed to be one of those special events that everyone in the neighborhood attended. Over the past two weeks, Jimmy's team had practiced numerous times.

Today, the Blue Sox were to play the previous year's league champion, Community Bank. Their ace pitcher, Larry Barnes, was the league's best pitcher. Jimmy knew that Larry would be sharper and even more powerful, now that he was twelve-years-old.

Every year, The Blue Sox were issued the same colors for their uniform: white with blue socks and a blue baseball hat. While getting dressed, Jimmy began to get a nervous feeling in his stomach. He wondered if everyone was feeling the same butterflies he was. Jillie came running into his room, also excited about opening day.

"Is the refreshment stand going to have ice cream today?" she asked.

"Every year at every game they have ice cream," said Jimmy. "I bet you they'll have it today as well."

"Oh good," she said with a sigh of relief. "Hurry up. Mom and Dad said they're ready to go."

Jimmy was fully dressed in his uniform. He sat down on his bed speaking out loud, as if he was speaking to A1-33.

"I'm nervous about today's game," he said. "I want to play well so badly. What if I let the team down? I just have to play well."

Jimmy shook his head in bewilderment. I'm talking to A1-33 as if the stadium seat can hear me, he thought.

Picking up his baseball shoes and glove, Jimmy left his bedroom. He suddenly heard a voice from behind say, "Just have fun today."

Jimmy stopped and whirled around toward his bedroom to see who had spoken to him. There was no one there, and the room was completely quiet. His eyes locked onto A1-33. Jimmy then turned and walked down the stairwell.

As he made his way downstairs, he saw his family waiting for him. "Did anyone just tell me to have fun today?" he asked.

Mom and Dad looked at each other with an expression of confusion, and immediately looked back at Jimmy.

"No, Jimmy," they said together.

Jillie rolled her eyes at her brother. "Come on. Let's get going."

The field was packed with fans. Even though the game wasn't for another hour, Jimmy got out of the car while Dad continued to search for parking.

Jimmy viewed the scoreboard and saw that the early game was in the bottom of the fifth. Trying to locate his team through the crowd, Jimmy scanned the perimeter of the field. He finally found Mike, Ricky, and Mr. Whitehill watching the game from outside the left field fence. Jimmy ran to join them. Mr. Whitehill greeted him with a smile, and within minutes the entire team was there.

"Grab a ball and warm up," directed Mr. Whitehill.

While Jimmy was throwing, he couldn't help but notice Community Bank's pitcher, Larry Barnes, warming up across the field. He sure can throw hard, Jimmy nervously thought to himself.

Mr. Whitehill called the team together, pointed to the field, and began to talk.

"This game is almost over, and soon it'll be our turn to take the field," he said. "We're the away team today, and we'll be in the third base dugout. Before you all go storming in there, let the team that's playing collect their equipment and leave. We've practiced hard over the last few weeks. I know we're ready for today's game. Community Bank is a strong opponent, but we have more talent and we're prepared to beat them. Let's play hard, and win the opener!"

The team cheered and the starting line-up for the game was read out as follows:

Joey Petruto	third base
Bobby Sharples	pitcher
Ricky Birk	shortstop
David Rockman	first base
Mike Laffey	catcher
Jimmy McNeil	second base
Stanley Johnson	left field
Keith Paeper	center field
Becky Reynolds	right field

"Now grab the equipment and let's head for the dugout," said Mr. Roshay.

Jimmy and the entire Blue Sox team did exactly as Mr. Roshay asked. As they got closer to the dugout, Community Bank, dressed in their green and white uniforms, made their way into the dugout on the first base line.

Jimmy looked up into the grandstand trying to locate his family. Fans from both teams were rustling to get seats. Most of the crowd was made up of parents smiling and greeting each other. As everyone started to sit down, Jimmy saw Sam sitting midway up the stands tipping the beak of his Yankee hat in his direction. Jimmy acknowledged Sam's greeting with a friendly wave.

Jimmy's dad noticed Sam sitting in front of him. He motioned for Sam to sit next to him and join the rest of the McNeil family.

As Jimmy followed his team into the dugout, he glanced toward Larry Barnes, which caused the nervous pit in his stomach to get worse. Jimmy tried to relax as he heard Mr. Whitehill remind his players of their signals, and the need to encourage each other during every play of the game.

Community Bank took the field, and the umpire yelled, "Play ball!"

Mr. Whitehill was in the third base coaching box, and Mr. Roshay was down the first base line. Joey stepped into the batter's box while every member of the Blue Sox stood up and cheered for their team's lead off hitter.

Larry Barnes wound up and delivered the first pitch of the season, a fastball right down the middle of the plate. Joey swung and missed.

"Strike one!" yelled the home plate umpire.

Community Bank and all their fans began cheering. Barnes had a smirk on his face as he set himself on the mound, and threw a pitch over Joey's head.

"Okay, Joey. It's got to be a good pitch," yelled Mr. Whitehill.

Joey backed out of the batter's box and took a deep breath. Barnes stood on the mound impatiently waiting for him to step up to the plate. Joey repositioned himself comfortably in the batter's box. He cocked his bat into place and waited for Larry's pitch. Barnes wound up and delivered another fastball right down the middle. Joey swung his bat around and made contact. It was a ground ball that found its way between the third baseman and shortstop. The ball rolled into left field for a base hit. Everyone in the Blue Sox dugout went wild.

Next up was Bobby Sharples. The Community Bank players all moved over two steps to the infield's right side, adjusting for the left handed batter. An agitated Larry Barnes threw his first pitch a little low. Bobby swung anyway, and hit a slow ground ball to second base. The second baseman fielded it cleanly, but rushed his throw to the shortstop, who was attempting to cover second base. The ball skipped into the outfield and Joey advanced to third while Bobby hustled to second base.

Barnes got so upset about the error he started yelling at his team's second baseman. Mr. Harrison, Community Bank's team manager, called out from the dugout, "Settle down, Larry."

Larry looked at his manager and frowned.

Ricky Birk took his turn at bat, and also swung at the first pitch. The ball popped up foul, and was easily caught by the third baseman for out number one.

David Rockman, the team's best hitter, walked up to the plate. The count went to 2-1. David's face contorted as he stared at the league's number one pitcher. Barnes wound up and fired the pitch. David's bat swung around as he cracked a long and powerful fly ball deep into left field. The ball banged against the left field fence. Joey and Bobby scored easily, and David landed at second with a stand up double. The Blue Sox fans cheered loudly in the stands.

As Joey and Bobby entered the dugout, they were greeted with enthusiasm by their teammates. Barnes was so disturbed, Community Bank's manager called time out and walked out to the pitcher's mound to speak with him.

Mike Laffey, the catcher, came up for the Blue Sox. Jimmy excitedly put on his helmet, selected his bat, and stepped into the on-deck circle. Jimmy looked through the fence and up toward the stands. Dad and Sam simultaneously gave him a smile. Jimmy half-smirked back as he felt himself becoming edgy.

"Strike one," yelled the umpire.

Jimmy turned around and watched Larry Barnes strike out Mike with three straight fastballs! Jimmy felt nervous as he made his way over to the plate. He could hear the muffled sound of the crowd cheering. His walk to the batter's box seemed to take forever. He was so nervous that everything around him looked like it was moving in slow motion.

"Let's go," yelled the umpire. "We don't have all day."

Jimmy stepped up to the plate. Barnes wound up and threw his first pitch. Jimmy was so anxious he swung, even though he clearly didn't see it. The ball skimmed off his bat and past the catcher.

"Foul ball," called the umpire.

At least I made contact, Jimmy thought to himself.

"Relax up there!" yelled Mr. Whitehill. "Just a base hit. That's all we need!"

The next pitch was way outside. Jimmy didn't swing, and the umpire called ball one. This made Jimmy relax a little bit. The third pitch was so fast, Jimmy didn't have time to even think about swinging. The ball echoed as it hit the catcher's glove. The next sound Jimmy heard was the umpire bellying out the words, "Strike two!"

With a one ball and two strike count, Jimmy was determined to hit the next pitch. As Barnes released the ball, Jimmy began his swing. The pitch was high, but it was too late, Jimmy had completed his swing and didn't even get close to the ball.

"Strike three!" hollered the umpire, and the top of the first inning was over. Jimmy looked at Barnes who started laughing at him.

Jimmy walked back to the dugout dejected. He peered up toward the stands and his dad gave him the "its okay" look, while Sam smiled and nodded. It made Jimmy feel a little better, but not much better. He quickly grabbed his glove and hustled out to second base.

The lead off hitter for Community Bank was a lefty. Mr. Whitehill directed Jimmy to move over a little closer to the first base line. Bobby Sharples wound up and threw his first pitch. The hitter swung and the ball smashed off his bat. A ground ball was hit between David Rockman at first and Jimmy at second. David moved to his right, but couldn't reach the ball. Jimmy was moving laterally to his left and came up with it. He quickly looked toward first, but there was no one to throw the ball to. David couldn't get back, and Bobby Sharples didn't get off the mound in time to cover the bag. Jimmy knew it would be a foot race to beat the batter to first. He took off immediately and could see that it was going to be close. Jimmy extended his leg and hit the closest part of first base with his right foot.

"He's out!" yelled the umpire.

As he headed back to his position at second base, Jimmy looked up to the stands behind his team's dugout. Mom and Dad were cheering for the play. Next to his dad stood Sam, who had a proud look on his face. Sam touched the beak of his hat and tipped it forward.

"Way to stay with the ball!" shouted Mr. Whitehill from the dugout, as Jimmy tossed the ball back to Bobby on the mound.

Bobby had trouble controlling his pitches and walked the next batter in four straight. There was one out and a runner on first. Larry Barnes came up to the plate. Mr. Whitehill called to the fielders to take a couple steps back. Besides being a good pitcher, Larry was also a good hitter.

Larry swung at Bobby's first pitch. It was a chopper to third. Joey handled it easily. Jimmy ran to cover second base for the double play. Joey was holding the ball waiting for Jimmy to get to the bag. When Jimmy finally got there, Joey threw the ball to him. Jimmy then extended his glove, and the ball barely beat the base runner. Jimmy turned to throw to first for the double play, but Barnes was already crossing first base. Jimmy held the ball and decided not to throw it.

Sharples ended the inning by striking out Community Bank's cleanup hitter and the defense hustled into the dugout.

The game moved along quickly. In the top of the third, Jimmy got a second chance at bat. On the first pitch, he popped the ball up foul to the catcher for an easy out. The Blue Sox held their 2-0 lead until the bottom of the fourth, when Community Bank scored its first run. In the top of the fifth, Joey, Mike, and Bobby went down consecutively. In the bottom of the fifth, Community Bank was coming up with their top batters.

Larry Barnes was the lead off hitter, and the count went to 3-1. Bobby went into a big wind up. He threw a fastball right down the middle. Larry swung his bat and sent the ball sailing into deep left center. Within seconds, the ball cleared the fence for a home run. Larry started his trip around the bases.

"I'll strike you out again next inning," taunted Larry as he passed second.

Jimmy looked at him and felt the pit return to his stomach.

Bobby Sharples seemed upset. Mr. Whitehill came out to the pitcher's mound to speak with him. Bobby listened to Mr. Whitehill's calming words. Mr. Whitehill then turned to the rest of the team and yelled, "let's have a little chatter out here for Bobby!"

The Blue Sox jumped in and supported their pitcher. Sounds of encouragement filled the park. Bobby pounded the ball in his mitt, stepped onto the pitcher's mound, and retired the next three batters in a row.

It was the top of the sixth inning, and the score was tied at two all. If neither team scored, they would have to play extra innings. Jimmy entered the dugout and flipped his glove onto the bench.

"Rockman, Laffey, and McNeil, you're up," called out Mr. Roshay.

This would be Jimmy's third chance at the plate, and his most crucial. He felt the palm of his hands begin to sweat as he picked up his bat and batter's helmet.

David Rockman stepped up to the plate and seemed as confident as ever. Why couldn't I be like that, thought Jimmy? On the mound, Barnes attempted to stare David down, but David just shined a smile that spread across his entire face.

Larry threw his first pitch. David's swing came around and plastered the ball into deep center field. Community Bank's center fielder headed straight back. There was no way he was going to catch the ball. The entire Blue Sox team jumped to their feet. The ball slammed against the center field fence. David rounded first and was chugging for second. David landed on second with another stand-up double.

Mike Laffey was up next, and Jimmy was on deck. The count on Mike went to 1-2. Barnes' next pitch looked like it was going to hit Mike. Laffey quickly dropped down to avoid contact. The ball went past the catcher and all the way to the backstop. Mr. Whitehill shouted to David to advance to third on the wild pitch. The Blue Sox's go-ahead run was now on third base.

The count was 2-2 on Mike. The next pitch was right down the middle. Mike swung and hit a chopper back to Barnes on the mound. David only took one step off third base, Barnes turned, and looked toward him. David wasn't going anywhere, so Barnes fired the ball to first base for the out.

Jimmy was so tense his body seemed frozen while in the on-deck circle. He was scared he would let the team down. As he started walking toward home plate, he heard a familiar voice softly say, "Relax Jimmy, just have fun."

Jimmy turned around, but no one was there. He continued toward home plate. Again, he heard a voice calling from behind: "Jimmy, this time have fun at bat."

In the background, Jimmy could hear his teammates calling out his name in support. As he stepped up to the plate, he looked down the third base line toward Mr. Whitehill.

"It must be your pitch, Jimmy," Mr. Whitehill said. "Swing only at a good one."

Barnes went into his big wind-up. As the ball left his hand, Jimmy's eyes stayed focused on the ball. He held up his swing as the pitch was moving toward the outside of the plate.

"Ball one," yelled the umpire.

"Good eye, Jimmy." Mr. Whitehill yelled.

The next pitch was high and inside for ball two. Jimmy looked toward Mr. Whitehill for a signal. He gave the take sign, meaning that Jimmy should not swing, no matter how good of a pitch was thrown. Unfortunately, Larry's third pitch was right down the middle for a called strike one.

The crowd was cheering loudly. Through the noise, Jimmy heard again, "Have fun."

Even though the voice seemed to come from inside his head, Jimmy understood its message.

He felt his whole body relax as Larry Barnes fired the next pitch. The ball was waist high moving on a straight path. Jimmy stepped up and swung. His eyes never came off the ball as his bat made contact. He hit a slow bouncing grounder to the right side of the infield. Jimmy ran down the first base path as fast as he could. The first baseman fielded the ball cleanly. He took two steps to his left and stepped on the bag. Jimmy was out. David Rockman was running from third to home. The first baseman pivoted and threw wildly. Community Bank's catcher was unable to catch the ball as David crossed the plate.

"Safe," howled the umpire, and the Blue Sox took the lead 3-2.

Jimmy ran to David, and together they trotted toward the dugout. The team was wild with excitement, as they greeted their teammates.

Stanley Johnson popped up for the third out, bringing an end to the top of the sixth. Jimmy hustled to get his glove. There was still half an inning to go. It was the bottom of Community Bank's line-up, but Mr. Whitehill was not about to let his team get over confident.

"These are the toughest three outs in baseball," he said as The Blue Sox poured out of the dugout and onto the field.

Bobby Sharples stepped on the pitcher's rubber determined to retire the next three batters. The first pitch he threw was hit back to him. Bobby easily fielded the chopper and threw the batter out at first. The next hitter popped up to Ricky at shortstop for out number two. Bobby then reached back and threw three straight blazing fastballs.

"Strike three!" yelled the ump, and the game was over.

Jimmy and his teammates converged on the mound and enthusiastically celebrated with their winning pitcher before returning to the dugout. Mr. Whitehill congratulated his happy team.

"Great game. I'm real proud of you," he said. "This was a big game for us, but if we're going to be champs this year, everyone must realize that this is only the beginning."

Every player on The Blue Sox cheered. They collected their equipment and left the playing field.

Jimmy's mom and dad were waiting for him. Mom grabbed her son and hugged him.

"Stop, Mom! You're embarrassing me." Jimmy said.

"Way to go, son. We're really proud of you and the team," said Dad.

Jimmy then looked up into the stands and saw Sam sitting alone. He walked over to him and asked him if he liked the game.

"It's been a long time since I enjoyed a game this much," Sam said. "Let me ask you a question. Did you like the game?"

"Well sure," Jimmy answered, a little unsure of why Sam was asking.

"Good. The whole idea of the game is to enjoy it."

"You mean have fun?" asked Jimmy cautiously.

"That's the way the game was meant to be played," answered Sam.

"Hey, Jimmy!" called Mr. Whitehill.

"You better go speak with your manager," encouraged Sam.

Jimmy turned and ran back to Mr. Whitehill, who was standing by the dugout.

"Nice game. You really hustled today, keep it up."

"Thanks, Mr. Whitehill. I will." Jimmy then ran back to the stands to find Sam, so they could finish their conversation, but Sam was gone. Jimmy looked down the road and saw him walking away.

"Sam," he called out loudly, unfortunately, Sam was already too far, and couldn't hear him.

Jimmy's father put his arm around his son's shoulder, and together they watched Sam walk further away.

"Don't worry. I think we're going to see a lot of Sam," said Dad.

"I hope so," said Jimmy.

CHAPTER 10

Jimmy didn't stop talking the entire ride home, even with the occasional interruptions by Jillie and her questions about the game.

"The team looks tough out there," Dad said. "I think you have a shot at the pennant this year."

"I hope each game isn't this close," Jimmy said.

"Why?" asked Mom. "I thought it was exciting. I would think playing in a close game is more fun."

Jimmy couldn't help but think how many times he'd heard the word "fun" today. Why does everybody keep saying that, he wondered?

Jillie opened the car door and dashed up the front steps. Jimmy was right behind her. Once inside, Jimmy flew up the stairs and into his room. He was about to toss his glove onto A1-33 when he stopped. His stadium seat was turned around facing the window again! Jimmy slowly walked over to the window with a confused look on his face. He picked up A1-33 and turned it around so that it was facing its usual position. Jimmy then knelt down on the ground and put his glove on the seat.

In a soft, private voice, Jimmy began to speak to his Yankee gift.

"We won today, but somehow I think you already know that," Jimmy said quietly. "It was a real close game. I played okay, not as well as I would have liked, but we still won. Sam was there. He said he enjoyed it and that it's been a long time since he'd seen such an exciting game."

That evening Jimmy's parents went out to dinner with friends. Jimmy was responsible for baby-sitting his sister. In between playing games with her, Jimmy spent most of the evening on the phone talking to Ricky and Mike about the day's Little League game. They discussed David Rockman's big hits, and tried to guess who would make the traveling All Star team. All three agreed that David would definitely be selected.

The boys talked about the Little League All-Star Tournament and how it's played during the summer, between neighboring leagues as well as against leagues from other cities. If a team keeps winning, they play against other state champions. The final tournament is played in Williamsport, Pennsylvania, and the best teams from around the world play in the final competition.

Jimmy' parents came home when he was on the phone talking. After Jimmy hung-up the phone, he went upstairs and sat in A1-33. He thought about playing in Williamsport, and how exciting it must be.

Jimmy fell asleep quickly that night. He barely remembered his head hitting the pillow. In his sleep, Jimmy heard the recognizable voice he now associated with A1-33.

"Jimmy, whenever there is a possible double-play ball, you must move closer to second base," said the voice. "Watch Scooter at short-stop, and Billy Martin playing second base."

Jimmy realized he was watching a Yankee game. He was sitting in A1-33. The fans around him were cheering loudly.

"Who's Scooter?" he asked.

Through the noise, A1-33 answered, "Phil Rizzuto. Jimmy, pay close attention. There's a man on first, Billy Martin has moved closer to the second base bag and has taken two steps back. He's now in a much better position to turn a double play. Watch what happens."

The batter was wearing a uniform that read "Senators." He was a right-handed batter. The Yankee pitcher wound up and delivered a fastball. The batter swung and hit a grounder to the shortstop. Scooter fielded the ball and tossed it to Billy Martin, who was approaching the second base bag. Martin stepped across the base and rocketed a throw to first for the double play.

The next thing Jimmy knew, the stadium was empty. He was stand-ing in the Yankee infield at second base. "You see, Jimmy, on a double-play situation you have to give yourself an edge."

Jimmy looked all around to locate where the voice of A1-33 was coming from. He saw nothing and continued to listen.

"Baseball is a thinking game. You must anticipate where you're go-ing to go when the ball is hit. Always think about the different scenarios, so you're prepared for every possibility. Now, let's practice different situations. You're playing second, there's a runner on first with one out. The ball's hit to the shortstop. Where do you go?"

"That's easy," answered Jimmy. "We just watched it. I go to second for the force and then throw to first."

"Good. Try this one," said the voice. "Bases loaded, no outs, and your team is up one run. Where do you position yourself, and what do you do with the ball if it comes to you?"

Jimmy thought for a short while.

"Play back and try to get the double play?" he asked unsure.

"No, Jimmy," returned the voice. "Move up on the edge of the in-field grass. There are no outs. You need a double play, but you want to eliminate the chance of the run scoring. Give the catcher the opportu-nity to throw to either third or first, wherever he can make the play."

The lessons seemed to go on for the longest time. Jimmy would position himself differently with each new situation. He looked up into the stands from second base. The stadium looked empty and lonely without anyone in it. It was getting dark and the stadium lights were turning on. Jimmy stared directly into them, and they became very bright. His eyes began to squint, and everything seemed out of focus. Then through the light, he saw Mom open the blinds to his window.

Jimmy's mom sat down on the bed next to her son. She looked down at the lower end of the bed and saw a small amount of fine dirt and grass lying next to Jimmy's uncovered feet.

"You know, young man, you should keep your sneakers or baseball shoes off the bed," she said. "You've gotten dirt on the sheets."

Jimmy sat up, rubbed his eyes, and looked to see what his mother was talking about. Jimmy knew he hadn't put his shoes on the bed.

"Were you going to sleep all morning?" Mom asked.

"I was in the middle of a dream," Jimmy answered.

"Probably about baseball," Mom said smiling.

Jimmy looked at Mom, then at the dirt and grass on his bed. With a knowing smile, he turned toward A1-33.

CHAPTER 11

It was game day. When the school bell rang at three o'clock, Jimmy jumped out of his seat and took off like a racecar through the class-room door. Without looking, he quickly turned the corner of the hall-way. By the time Jimmy realized he was about to crash into someone, it was too late. He felt the thump of the collision and books went flying everywhere.

"Where are you going, turkey?" Larry Barnes said in a threatening voice.

"Sorry Larry, it was just an accident," said Jimmy softly.

"Yeah, so was your win last Saturday," Larry sneered.

A crowd started to gather, and a few of Larry's friends began to laugh. Jimmy became embarrassed.

"We won the game, and you were the losing pitcher," Jimmy snapped back.

"You had nothing to do with the win, McNeil," said Larry. "If that little ground ball you hit was played properly, Rockman wouldn't have scored. Matter of fact, you were lucky you even hit that cheap little grounder."

Jimmy could sense the crowd getting larger. Larry had put him on the spot. Everyone was looking at him and waiting to see if he would return a verbal punch or let Barnes walk away the victor.

"Face it, Larry, your pitching record is 0 and 1," Jimmy said ner-vously. "So much for the return of the All-Star."

Larry became enraged. He raised his arms as if he was about to push Jimmy into the school lockers. Jimmy quickly put his arms up in an effort to thwart the attack and slow Barnes down.

Suddenly, there was a thunderous voice: "Hey Barnes! Want to pick on me?"

Larry Barnes paused, and everyone watching went silent. Jimmy saw David Rockman approaching with a fierce look on his face.

"Come on big shot," said David. "I saw what happened. McNeil told you it was an accident and apologized. Now pick up your books and go home. Barnes picked up his things and hurried off.

Jimmy bent down and picked up his books.

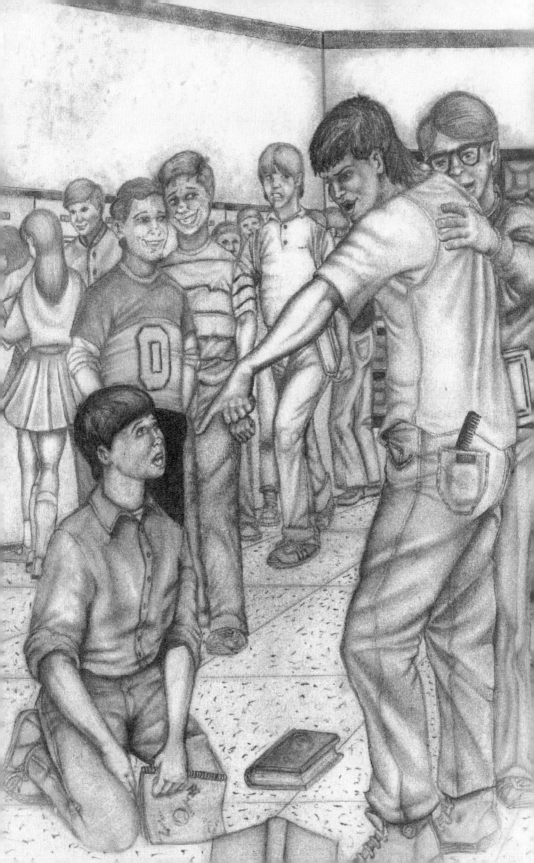

"Thanks, David," said Jimmy.

"Don't worry about it," returned David. "Barnes can be a jerk sometimes. It's too bad, because he's a good ballplayer."

Jimmy nodded in agreement. The Blue Sox's first and second baseman walked out of school together.

"What time are you going to the field?" David asked.

"About 5:30. How about you?"

"The same time. I'll meet you there so we can warm up together."

Both boys began walking away.

"Hey, McNeil!" David yelled, turning around. "You know your ground ball did drive me in!"

"I don't think it drove you in. I hit it so slow, I think it rolled you in," Jimmy yelled back.

David laughed and waved as he continued to walk home.

It must be nice to be as tough as David, Jimmy thought to himself as he walked home.

CHAPTER 12

Jimmy walked to Welty Park with Mike and Ricky. Tonight, they were playing the Main Street Grill, who had lost their opener the previous weekend. The three boys were feeling confident they could win tonight's game. As they entered the gates of the ballpark, they saw David Rockman.

"You going to pound the ball against the fence again?" Ricky asked David.

"Only if you get on base before me," David answered with a smile.

"Get loose, guys," Mr. Whitehill directed from the first base dugout.

Jimmy grabbed the ball and held it up to David. Rockman nodded his head in the direction of the infield as a sign to begin throwing. Ricky paired up with Joey Petruto, and Mr. Whitehill took Mike Laffey into the outfield on the first base line to warm up Charlie Owens, who would be the starting pitcher.

Charlie was eleven-years-old and was the team's number two pitcher in the rotation. Bobby was going to play center field; otherwise, the starting line-up would remain the same as it was on opening day.

It was approaching game time. Jimmy saw his mom and Jillie entering from the parking lot. Mom waved her son over.

"Dad's going to be late," she said.

"Why?" Jimmy asked.

"Overtime at the stadium, but he'll be here later in the game."

As Mom walked back to where Jillie was standing, she spotted Sam. Jimmy watched as his mother exchanged a friendly hello with Sam. Sam smiled, then knelt down and gave Jillie a present. Jimmy couldn't see what it was, but his mom and sister were making a big fuss over it. Sam escorted Jimmy's mother and Jillie to their seats.

Sam then walked over to Jimmy. Jimmy noticed that in addition to his Yankee hat, Sam was wearing a 1940's style Yankee warm-up jacket.

"Hi, Sam," Jimmy said enthusiastically.

"Hello, Jimmy. Ready for tonight's game?" Sam asked.

"I think so. I just hope I hit the ball better today."

"Just relax at the plate. Stay calm and keep your eye on the ball."

Jimmy nodded in agreement.

"What have you learned about baseball this week?" Sam asked.

Jimmy wasn't sure what Sam was asking, so he remained silent.

"Think about it. What did you learn in practice this week?" Sam asked again.

"We didn't have practice this week," Jimmy answered.

"Your team didn't, but you did," Sam said smiling. "Remember, you have the best coach in the game. Just think about it."

Sam then touched the beak of his hat and nodded as he walked back to the stands to join Jimmy's mom and sister.

Suddenly, it hit Jimmy like a ton of bricks. Sam knew about his dreams and the practices at Yankee Stadium! But how could he know, Jimmy wondered.

"Hey, Jimmy! Come on, it's game time," Ricky hollered.

Jimmy looked toward Ricky and saw his team taking the field for the top half of the first inning. He quickly ran to his position at second base. Charlie Owens pitched a great first inning. He struck out two and walked one. The Main Street Grill's clean up hitter popped up to Ricky at shortstop for the third out.

In the bottom half of the first, Robert Mendel took the mound for the Main Street Grill. Joey Petruto swung at the first pitch and led off the inning with a base hit up the middle. Bobby Sharples then followed with a hard line drive, which was caught by the third baseman. Ricky took his turn in the batters box. Mendel released his pitch, the ball moved quickly to the inside. Ricky tried to move away from the ball, but he couldn't in time. Mr. Whitehill went running over to see how he was. Ricky quickly waved his hand to show that he was hit by the ball but still okay.

It was first and second with one out. David slowly walked up to the plate. The count went to 3-1. Rockman set himself in the batters box. Mendel delivered his pitch. Rockman swung and blasted the ball into deep left field. The Blue Sox's whole team stood up in the dugout. The ball easily sailed over the fence. The shot gave the Sox an early three run lead. David crossed the plate and was mobbed with congratulations from his teammates.

Jimmy realized he better grab a bat and helmet and get into the on-deck circle. Mike quickly walked on four straight pitches. Jimmy moved toward home plate. Mr. Whitehill walked halfway down the third base path and called out to Jimmy: "Mendel's throwing wild. Wait until he delivers a strike before swinging!"

Jimmy entered the batter's box understanding Mr. Whitehill's every word. Mendel threw the first pitch right down the middle for a strike, though.

Jimmy was too anxious. He kept calculating what his batting average would be if he got a hit. This would make me one for four, which is a batting average of 250. All of a sudden, Jimmy saw Mendel throw the ball. He didn't feel ready, but the pitch appeared to be good. As he started to swing, the ball moved inside. The handle of his bat made slight contact with the ball and skipped to the backstop.

"Foul ball," called the umpire, and the count went to 0-2.

Jimmy heard Mr. Whitehill encouraging him, "Keep your eye on the ball, Jimmy. You can do it."

Mendel's pitch came in, and Jimmy swung. The ball popped up into the air right back to the pitcher's mound. Mendel handled the ball easily, and Jimmy was out.

As he entered the team's dugout, David Rockman walked up to him. "Go easy, Jimmy," said David. "You're trying too hard."

Jimmy half-smiled and said, "Thanks. That was a great shot you hit"

"I just got lucky," David humbly responded.

Stanley Johnson quickly grounded out to short, putting an end to the bottom of the first.

The next two innings were scoreless. Owens was pitching a great game, and only gave up one hit through the top of the fourth. Jimmy had fielded two balls, both cleanly. In the bottom of the fifth, Jimmy would lead his team off at the plate. As he exited the dugout, Jimmy turned left and saw his father. Dad waved to his son and Jimmy waved back. Sam looked toward Jimmy, his right hand pointed to his eyes. Jimmy knew Sam was telling him to keep his eye on the ball.

Jimmy took Sam's advice. Mendel's control was off, and Jimmy waited for a good pitch. He took only one called strike before he got four balls and was awarded a walk to first base.

"There you go, Jimmy," shouted Mr. Whitehill. "Way to wait it out!"

Jimmy trotted down to first. He had just gotten on base for the first time this year. Standing on the bag, Jimmy looked up into the stands. Sam sat there with a smile on his face, while his father gave his son the thumbs up.

Stanley Johnson came up to the plate. From first base, Jimmy looked toward Mr. Whitehill and saw that he had given Stanley a bunt sign. Stanley bunted the next pitch, and the ball began bouncing toward third. Jimmy took off and ran as hard as he could for second. The third baseman fielded the ball, but the rest of the infield became confused. The third baseman threw to second, unaware nobody had stepped up to cover the base!

"Third base, Jimmy. Third base," yelled Mr. Whitehill.

Jimmy ran fast and hard. As he approached third, Mr. Whitehill put his hands up in the air to slow Jimmy down. The ball was thrown to the catcher, and Stanley Johnson advanced to second.

"Nice running." Mr. Whitehill said. "There are no outs."

Becky Reynolds came up to bat. She knocked the first pitch delivered by Mendel right up the middle.

"Go!" yelled Mr. Whitehill to Jimmy.

Jimmy took off like a flash and crossed home plate in time to see the ball being thrown back into the infield. Stanley held at third, and Becky stood safely on first. Becky waved at Jimmy as he entered the dugout and Jimmy waved back as if to say thanks! Mike and Ricky came up to him immediately.

"Way to run!" Mike said.

"Hey Jimmy!" blurted David Rockman. "You can really move."

Jimmy looked up, and smiled.

By the time the inning was over, Jimmy's team had scored another two runs. They knocked Robert Mendel out of the game, and the Main Street Grill had to bring in a new pitcher. Going into the top of the sixth, the Sox were holding a 6-0 lead.

Charlie Owens struck out the first batter, and went to a full count with the next batter before throwing high and outside for ball four. There was a runner on first with one out.

Jimmy remembered baseball was a thinking game. You must anticipate what you're going to do when the ball is hit, Jimmy thought to himself. Realizing there was a right-handed hitter, Jimmy moved over to his right, closer to second base. Then he took two steps back. Jimmy crouched down in his infield position and encouraged Charlie on the mound.

"Come on, Charlie! No hitter!" he called out.

Soon the whole team was cheering for Charlie. Charlie wound up and delivered the pitch.

Bang! The ball was hit to Ricky at shortstop. In three quick steps, Jimmy was over to second base. His mind flashed back to Yankee Stadium, and he pictured Billy Martin stepping across the bag after receiving the ball from Phil Rizzuto. Jimmy caught a perfect toss from Ricky and then came across the second base bag. He pivoted and threw a bullet to David Rockman, who had extended his glove in anticipation. The ball beat the batter to first by a full step.

"Out!" yelled the umpire.

What a finish! The Sox ended the game with a double play. A smiling Mr. Whitehill waved the team in. Jimmy hustled toward the dugout and saw Sam in the stands nodding his head and touching the beak of his hat. Jimmy touched the beak of his hat in return.

"We got great pitching out of Charlie Owens, and of course that big home run from Rockman," said Mr. Whitehill.

Everyone started to cheer for both players.

"And how about that great game-ending double-play between Birk and McNeil," Mr. Whitehill added.

Ricky and Jimmy looked at each other and laughed.

"Now hold on, guys," warned Mr. Whitehill. "Remember, you're playing good ball, but we've only won two games. There are thirteen more to go. Let's play each game one at a time."

The entire team became quiet. Mr. Whitehill had made his point. They must not let themselves become overconfident. Mr. Roshay announced that the team should meet at 12:30 on Saturday for their one o'clock game. One by one, the Blue Sox piled out of the dugout.

Jimmy's family was waiting for him as he exited through the playing field gate.

"Great game, Jimmy," said Dad.

"You were wonderful!" added Mom.

"You played smart tonight," said Sam.

"Thanks," Jimmy said to everyone.

"How about we all get something to eat?" Jimmy's Dad asked.

Jimmy quickly looked toward Sam. Jimmy's father knew exactly what Jimmy was thinking.

"Yes, Jimmy," Dad said smiling. "Sam's joining us today."

CHAPTER 13

Jimmy loved going to Burgerville after games. It was a family tradition. He thought the food was great, and he often saw players and families from other teams.

The McNeil family and Sam found a corner table at the back of the restaurant. Once everyone was seated, Jillie placed a small box she'd been carrying on the table.

"Look what Sam gave me, " she announced.

Jillie opened the box, and showed Jimmy a small, wooden framed picture of Shirley Temple.

Peering across the table, Jimmy looked at the picture. He smiled slightly.

"That's nice, Jillie," Jimmy said in a relaxed voice.

"I think you better take a closer look at that picture, Mr. Big Shot," Mom said.

Jimmy realized his mom wanted him to be more considerate to his sister. Jimmy zoomed in at the picture and saw Shirley Temple sitting in seat A1-33 at Yankee Stadium!

"Wow! Jillie, let me see that!" Jimmy blurted.

"Sure, but be very careful with it," Jillie instructed. "This picture belongs to me."

Everyone laughed, and then Jimmy turned toward Sam.

"Did Shirley Temple really watch a game sitting in A1-33?" Jimmy asked.

Sam nodded.

"Please, Sam, tell me the story again," Jillie said.

Sam paused before beginning. "It was 1936, and Shirley Temple was in New York City filming a movie. As everyone knows by now, A1-33 was Mrs. Gehrig's seat. Well, Mrs. Gehrig was a big movie fan. When she heard Shirley Temple was in New York, she contacted the film director, and invited Miss Temple and some friends to come watch the game."

"That must have been fun," said Mom.

"It was," continued Sam. "Shirley had a great time, and she autographed this picture and sent it to me. It was her way of saying thank you for showing her around the stadium."

"This must be a cherished possession of yours. It wouldn't be right for Jillie to accept it," Mom told Sam

"I enjoyed watching Jillie at the game last Saturday. She reminded me of Shirley Temple at Yankee Stadium," said Sam gently. "It's worth watching the twinkle in her eye. She's a good sister for coming to all of Jimmy's games. She deserves something special."

Everyone at the table smiled, including the waitress, who was standing by ready to take their order.

After dinner, the McNeil family dropped Sam off at the train stop.

"Are you sure we can't take you all the way home?" Dad asked.

Sam had insisted upon taking the train. It was late when they finally arrived back at the house. Jillie had fallen asleep in the back seat of the car, with her hand clutched around the picture of Shirley Temple. Dad carried her inside, and Jimmy went directly to his room to prepare for bed.

To Jimmy's astonishment, A1-33 was turned around facing the window! Jimmy turned the seat back around and sat on the floor in front of it.

"I finally realized tonight," said Jimmy quietly, "that there's something really special about you and Sam. I guess you've always made people happy."

"Jimmy, who are you talking to?" asked Mom from the hallway.

"Just myself," returned Jimmy.

"It's late. Wash up and go to sleep," she replied.

While lying in bed, Jimmy thought about Sam and A1-33. He was confused. He needed to talk with Sam alone. But how, he wondered.

CHAPTER 14

It was Friday, and school had just recessed for the weekend. Jimmy had three hours to find Sam. He ran to the station to catch a train to Yankee Stadium. The ride felt like it took forever. It was 3:30 when Jimmy finally got to the 161st Street stop.

Jimmy knew Sam lived close to the stadium, so he went directly there. Hoping to find Sam, Jimmy sat on the curb across the street from the players' entrance.

It was getting late, and there was still no sign of Sam. As Jimmy was preparing to leave, he got a weird ringing in his ear. He shook his head trying to stop it, but it didn't work. Without warning, the ringing became the familiar voice of A1-33: "Pop's Candy Store, corner of 161st and Jerome Avenue."

As Jimmy was repeating out loud what A1-33 had just said, a kid dressed in baggy pants and wearing the same old-fashioned Yankee jacket Sam wore, said, "Pop's Candy Store? What about it?"

"Where is it?" Jimmy asked.

"It's on 161st street, one block down," the kid explained. "You'll see it on the corner of Jerome Avenue."

Jimmy thanked the strangely dressed kid, who smiled and then turned and walked down the street. Jimmy ran all the way. A few minutes later, he was standing in front of a soda shop and candy store. There was a small sign over the door that read: "Pop's." As Jimmy entered, he noticed the place looked old.

There was a man behind the soda counter wearing a white apron and a little white cap on his head. As Jimmy looked around him, he saw spinning stools in front of the counter, and walls filled with Yankee pictures, most of them bearing autographs. Over to the right, there were four green booths along the wall. Sam sat in the third booth from the door. From afar, Jimmy watched Sam comfortably drinking a cup of coffee and reading the newspaper.

Without looking up, Sam began to speak: "Have a seat, Jimmy. I've been wondering when we were going to talk."

Jimmy slid into the seat across the table.

"Yeah, me too," said Jimmy.

Sam looked up from his newspaper wearing his usual smile.

"Would you like something to eat?" Sam asked.

"A soda would be great," Jimmy answered.

"Hey, Pop. How about a soda for my friend?"

Pop came over to the table and asked, "Are you a Yankee fan, son?"

"He's a Yankee fan with a big Yankee dream," Sam said.

Pop nodded and went behind the counter.

"Sam, since Dad brought home A1-33, I've had some crazy dreams," said Jimmy.

"Which ones are crazy, Jimmy?" asked Sam. "The one about your baseball glove or Bobby Richardson practicing in Yankee Stadium?"

"How do you know about them?" Jimmy asked with a surprised look.

"A1-33 communicates to the both of us, which allows me to be there if you need help," said Sam.

"But Sam, it's a stadium seat. How can it communicate to us? I don't understand," said Jimmy with a puzzled look on his face.

"A1-33 is more than just a stadium seat. Like you and I, A1-33 also shares a love for the game of baseball and the New York Yankees."

"I still don't understand. I dreamt I was grown up and playing for the Yankees."

"I know," Sam said. "That is your dream, isn't it? To play for the Yankees?"

"Yes," said Jimmy.

"Only you can make your dreams come true. A1-33 is your guide and your coach."

"You mean A1-33 is the answer to my dreams?"

Sam leaned across the table.

"No, you're the answer, Jimmy," Sam said. "The answer of your own dreams and the dream of A1-33."

Jimmy shook his head in further confusion.

"Some day it will all make sense to you. Through experience you'll gain a better understanding," explained Sam. "In the meantime, A1-33 is a special friend to the both of us. Listen to A1-33. Remember all that he'll teach you in the years to come. Don't expect all the answers at once. The most important thing for you right now is to learn through A1-33."

"Learn baseball?"

Sam took a long pause, and then said: "There's more to learn than baseball. What have you learned so far?"

"Well, I've learned that in baseball it's important to think," said Jimmy.

"Good. What else?"

"I learned that the center field monuments are being fenced in."

Sam chuckled then asked, "What did you learn during your first Little League game?"

"Playing baseball is suppose to be fun!" Jimmy announced.

"Yes," Sam replied. "That's one of the most important lessons that you'll learn. It's a game, a great game, Jimmy, and games are meant to be fun."

"Do the pros feel that way?"

"The great ones do. The superstars, as your generation calls them, only remain great when they keep the original purpose of the game in mind."

Jimmy nodded. He finally had a better understanding of what Sam was trying to tell him. Jimmy then caught a glimpse of the wall clock, which read 5:15. He jumped out of the booth.

"I better get home," Jimmy said. "I can't be late for dinner. Will you be at the game tomorrow?"

"I can't make it," Sam said with regret. "Tomorrow's April 18th. It's a busy day for me, but I'll be at the next one."

Jimmy waved good-bye to Sam, and hurried down the street to the subway station. Just before he got to the entrance he looked back and saw Sam watching him. Sam tipped the beak of his Yankee hat and then turned away. Jimmy watched him cross the street. When he reached the other side a bus went by. When the bus had passed, Sam was gone.

CHAPTER 15

*If we're going to win the pennant, we've got to start
thinking we're not as good as we think we are.*

–Casey Stengel

It was Saturday, and Jimmy arrived at Welty Park at exactly 12:30.
The Blue Sox, led by Bobby Sharples on the mound, were about to play
the Cross County Cubs. The Cubs had lost their first two games. Before the game, Mr. Whitehill had conducted a fielding drill. The game
was scheduled to start at one o'clock, which didn't leave any time for
batting practice. This was the third game, and Jimmy's only thought
was his 0 for 4 batting average. He had been playing well in the field,
but Jimmy knew he had to start hitting.

The first three innings of the game were scoreless and moving
quickly. Jimmy had three plays at second base, and handled them cleanly.
His first time at bat, he grounded out to the first baseman.

In the fourth, Jimmy was the Sox's third batter up. Rockman led off
the inning with a hard hit ground ball to third. It bounced off the
baseman's glove, and Rockman was safe at first. Mike Laffey came to
the plate and popped up to the shortstop for the first out. As he entered
into the batter's box, Jimmy looked toward Mr. Whitehill for a signal.
Jimmy received the bunt sign. The pitcher went into his wind-up. As he
released the ball, Jimmy quickly lowered his bat even with his waist.
His right hand slid up the bat and he moved it toward the ball, but missed.

"Strike one," Jimmy heard the umpire yell.

Jimmy looked toward Mr. Whitehill, who again gave the bunt signal. Stay calm and don't fish after a bad one, Jimmy thought to himself.

The next pitch was in the strike zone. Jimmy moved his bat forward
to meet the ball. It banged off the bat and popped up to the pitcher for
an easy out. With his head down, Jimmy walked into the dugout. He
was so disappointed. Now he was 0 for 6. He didn't think he'd ever get a
hit.

The half-inning was over when Stanley Johnson struck out on a 2-2
pitch, stranding Rockman on first.

In the bottom of the fourth, the Cross County Cubs had their top of
the line-up at bat. The lead off batter got on base safely and now Al

Bonsard was up next. He was a lefty and had grounded out to Jimmy in the top of the first.

Think about the play, Jimmy thought. Jimmy moved to the left, knowing that Al was a pull hitter. Jimmy went through different situations in his mind. He knew the most important thing was to try to get the lead runner out at second.

The count was at 2-1 when Al hit a slow chopper down the first base line. Rockman and Sharples both charged the ball, this left first base uncovered. Jimmy ran over to cover it. Bobby came up with the ball. He looked to throw to second, but he knew he wouldn't beat the runner. Bobby quickly turned to first, where Jimmy was covering the bag. Sharples fired the ball to him for the out. The base runner, Cameron Razzo, advanced to second. Jimmy looked toward the runner and then called time out.

The next batter for the Cross County Cubs slammed the first pitch into left field for a base hit. Their third base coach waved Razzo home. Johnson threw the ball left of Mike Laffey at home plate and the runner scored easily. The batter advanced to second on a wild throw, and Jimmy could see Bobby was getting upset.

"Just relax, Bobby," suggested Jimmy. "You're pitching a great game. We'll get them next inning."

The Cubs clean-up hitter, a righty, was up to bat. Again, Jimmy started to think about the next play. I need to hold the runner at second and throw the batter out if I get the ball, he thought. Jimmy took two steps to his right. He crouched down in position and watched Sharples toss his pitch. The clean-up hitter started to swing as the ball approached home plate. The ball came crashing off the bat. It was a line drive up the middle.

Jimmy was leaning to his right and started moving in the direction of the ball. As quickly as he could, he extended his glove hand and caught the ball just before it landed on the ground. Jimmy saw the runner on second had taken a few steps toward third. Jimmy composed himself and quickly stepped across the second base bag for the third out. Jimmy ended the inning with a double-play, all by himself!

The whole infield came running over to Jimmy to congratulate him on his great play. Mr. Whitehill greeted Jimmy with a pat on the back, and motioned for the team to get back into the dugout.

"Okay everyone, listen up," said Mr. Whitehill. "We're down one nothing and it's late in the game. Let's put a few runs on the board!"

Charged by Jimmy's play, the team scored two runs, highlighted by

Bobby Sharples' triple. The Blue Sox took a 2-1 lead.

The next two innings were shutout ball. The Sox won the game and their record moved to 3 and 0. This gave them sole possession of first place. Mr. Whitehill gave his usual post-game pep talk.

"Every team is improving, and you must take each opponent seriously," said Mr. Whitehill.

Jimmy and his teammates stayed and watched the second game. Community Bank was playing Main Street Grill. Jimmy and Ricky were both hungry and decided to go to the refreshment stand to get a bite to eat. Along the way, they passed Larry Barnes who was entering the field.

"Nice bunt, McNeil. Have you gotten a hit yet?" Barnes asked sarcastically.

"We're in first place, Barnes," Jimmy answered.

"We'll see what happens next time we play," said Barnes.

"Come on, Jimmy, let's get going," interjected Ricky.

Community Bank destroyed Main Street Grill 8 to 2. Their record was now 2 and 1, right behind the Sox. Ricky and Jimmy walked home together after the game.

"You're playing great," said Ricky to Jimmy.

"My fielding is okay, but I'm still batting zero," returned Jimmy. "You heard Barnes. Everybody knows it."

"Maybe all you need is some batting practice."

"Some? I need a lot."

The two buddies laughed.

It took Jimmy a long time to fall asleep that evening. He kept thinking what Barnes had said about his bunting. Jimmy turned and gazed toward A1-33. Feeling restless, he got out of bed and sat in the chair. Surprisingly, he found himself sitting in Yankee Stadium.

"Grab a bat and go to home plate," he heard A1-33 say.

Jimmy climbed out of the stands and picked up a bat that looked just like the one he used in Little League. On the mound was a pitching machine.

"When you're bunting to advance a runner, your goal is to sacrifice yourself as an out. You want everyone in the ballpark to know what you're doing. Square your body around so you're facing the pitcher," said A1-33.

Jimmy listened and followed all of A1-33's directions.

"Now keep your left hand on the handle of the bat and slide your right hand up to a little more than halfway. Make sure the barrel of the bat is resting between your index finger and your thumb. Do not close your hand around the bat, or the ball will hit your fingers. When the ball comes in, guide the bat so it drops the ball in the direction you want it to go. Now let's practice with the pitching machine."

A1-33 continued to instruct Jimmy on how to improve this skill.

"Why do the pros dip their bats quickly when they're bunting?" Jimmy asked.

"They only do that when they're trying to bunt for a base hit," returned A1-33. "You'll learn that in a few years; right now, concentrate on sacrifice bunts. It's one of the basic skills of the game. You'll need to learn all of the basic skills to be ready."

"Ready for what?" Jimmy asked.

"Ready to make your dream come true."

Jimmy began bunting balls down the first base line, then the third base line, then between the pitcher's mound and the bases. The bunting drill must have gone on for hours. When Jimmy woke up the following morning, he couldn't wait to try out his new skill at practice.

CHAPTER 16

Jimmy got to the ballpark a little early. He was eager to take batting practice and actually try bunting as A1-33 had taught him. While he waited at the field, Jimmy's mind floated back to his conversation with Sam the previous Friday.

"Hello, Jimmy," said Mr. Whitehill.

"Oh, hello, Mr. Whitehill," said Jimmy.

"You seemed a million miles away. What were you thinking about?"

"Nothing in particular. I must've been daydreaming."

"I'm glad you're here early. I wanted to talk to you. At the end of the season, the league managers get together and choose a traveling All-Star team."

Jimmy's eyes popped out of his sockets as he listened.

"You're playing as good as any infielder I've ever seen in this league. You have all the moves and your fielding is great."

"Thanks," Jimmy said proudly.

"But," Mr. Whitehill interrupted, "you seem to be having trouble hitting the ball. If you're to make the All-Star team, we're going to have to improve your batting."

His manager's comments crushed him. Mr. Whitehill understood his second baseman's emotions. He urged Jimmy to not get down on himself.

"You have a lot of talent, and we have time to improve your batting average," Mr. Whitehill added.

"I have a zero batting average," said Jimmy.

"Just relax. You seem too tense when you're batting. Try to be as comfortable at the plate as you are on the field."

When the rest of the team showed up, practice began with fielding drills, followed by batting practice. Each player took twenty swings. Jimmy hit mostly pop ups or slow ground balls. He tried relaxing while keeping his eye on the ball. After he took about fifteen swings, Jimmy could have sworn he heard A1-33 saying, "Bunt, Jimmy. Bunt."

Jimmy stepped away from the plate and heard it again.

Jimmy stepped back in the box, and on the next pitch, he squared around just as A1-33 had taught him. Joey was playing third, and he came moving in. Jimmy followed the pitch all the way in and then laid down a perfect bunt between Joey and the pitcher's mound.

Mr. Whitehill came out of the dugout, and said, "Jimmy, that was a great bunt. Let's see another."

On the next pitch, Jimmy bunted down the first base line. He continued to bunt a few more times.

"Okay, next batter!" yelled Mr. Whitehill.

Jimmy flipped off his helmet and grabbed his glove. Mr. Whitehill called out to him.

"Jimmy, you're bunting much better today than you did yesterday," he said.

"I had a lot of practice," returned Jimmy.

A strange look came over his manager's face as Jimmy ran out to the field.

Lying in bed that night, Jimmy started thinking about his conversations with Mr. Whitehill. He turned to A1-33 and said out loud: "If I could start hitting, I'd have a shot at making the All-Star team."

Jimmy got up to sit in A1-33. He had come to enjoy sitting in the box seat, where he could pretend like he was watching a Yankee game, or sometimes just think about things.

All of a sudden, Jimmy found himself in Yankee Stadium sitting in A1-33! The stadium looked different. He immediately looked toward center field to see if the Monuments were there, but they weren't. The center field billboard was advertising a Micromatic Razor. What in the world is a Micromatic Razor, Jimmy thought to himself.

"Jimmy," spoke A1-33. "There's someone I would like you to meet. He's here to help you get out of your batting slump."

Jimmy noticed a ballplayer walking toward him from first base. The uniform he was wearing looked old-fashioned. It was big and heavy and didn't seem comfortable. His baseball socks showed very little white, not like the players he saw on TV. Also, his hat looked like the one that Sam wore.

The ballplayer told Jimmy he would find his bat over by the dugout.

"Why don't you grab it and meet me by home plate," he said to Jimmy.

Jimmy didn't move right away. As the ballplayer turned around, he saw the number four on his back. A tingling feeling climbed up Jimmy's back as he thought about whom he was with.

Jimmy heard A1-33 say, "Go ahead, Jimmy. You're about to take batting practice with Lou Gehrig."

In disbelief, Jimmy got up from his seat and slowly walked down the steps and onto the field. His eyes were fixed on the baseball legend.

Jimmy joined him at home plate.

"Jimmy, in August of 1938, I was in a bad hitting slump," said Mr. Gehrig. "Toward the end of the season, my average dropped to .270. As you know, it's not fun being in a batting slump."

Jimmy nodded.

"What are you trying to do about yours?" Lou asked.

"I'm trying to keep my eye on the ball and relax," said Jimmy. "Everyone tells me I need to relax."

"Do you think you need to relax?"

"I'm not sure. I do feel nervous when I get up to bat."

"In one of my slumps, I came up to the plate with two men on. Do you know what I did?"

"No, sir," Jimmy responded.

"I bunted," Lou explained.

"You did?"

"Everyone was stunned, but I bunted for one reason and one reason only. I needed to feel confident I could control my bat."

Jimmy listened to every word that came out of Lou Gehrig's mouth.

"Hitting the baseball is a combination of technique and skill," explained Mr. Gehrig. "But what's more important is confidence."

Lou Gehrig then stepped into the batter's box, and Jimmy backed away. On the pitcher's mound was another Yankee player in the same uniform.

"Come on, Lefty!" Lou yelled. "Throw a few over here so I can work with Jimmy on his hitting."

Lou Gehrig turned toward Jimmy.

"Watch my stance and swing, Jimmy. I keep my back foot still," said Mr. Gehrig, "and I step with my front foot. This transfers the power while keeping my balance. My eyes never leave the ball, and my swing stays level."

Jimmy watched as the Yankee great slammed balls into right field.

"Now its your turn," said Lou to Jimmy.

Jimmy got up to the plate. Mr. Gehrig moved Jimmy's legs and changed his stance a little bit.

"You look good," said Mr. Gehrig. "But how does it feel?"

Jimmy smiled, "It'll feel real good if I hit the ball."

Lou Gehrig then waved to the pitcher to start throwing. On the first pitch, Jimmy hit a ground ball to the left side of the infield. Lefty Gomez kept throwing, and Jimmy continued to hit ground balls.

"Don't worry about where they're going," Lou Gehrig said. "Just concentrate on making contact."

On the next pitch, Jimmy hit a line drive down the left field line.

"Good hit!" encouraged Mr. Gehrig.

Batting practice continued. After swinging at about 50 pitches, Lou Gehrig waved to the Yankee pitcher to stop. He put his arm around Jimmy's shoulders and walked him back to A1-33.

"Have a seat, Jimmy," said Mr. Gehrig.

"Yes, sir," returned Jimmy.

"You're not going to hit safely every time you get up to the plate. Just try to hit the ball properly. Eventually, they'll start landing in the right places. The most important thing you can remember at any level of the game is confidence."

Jimmy nodded.

"One last thing, Jimmy," added Mr. Gehrig. "Your dad told you something that's very important. He taught you that to be the best, you have to want to be the best. Follow that advice. Then you can make it happen."

Lou Gehrig became blurry. Jimmy's eyes started to open wide, as he saw his dad looking over him.

"Son, it's time to wake up for school," Dad said.

How did I get in bed? When did I fall asleep? Jimmy asked himself.

"Everything okay?" Dad questioned.

Jimmy thought about his dream and flashed a bright smile.

"Everything's great Dad," he answered. "Just great."

Jimmy's dad winked at his son and then walked out of the room.

Jimmy got up and sat on the edge of his bed looking at A1-33. That was the best dream I've ever had, he thought.

CHAPTER 17

Thursday evening, the Sox were playing the last place team, Eastside Service Station. Their record was 0-3, but the team was anxious for a win. Jimmy's entire team felt this would be an easy game. Mr. Whitehill continually told them to take every team seriously, regardless of the team's record. He didn't want them to become over confident.

Jimmy began warming up on the third base line with Ricky.

"Hey, Jimmy! Look over in the stands," said Ricky. "Isn't that the strange guy that's been coming to our games?"

Jimmy looked to his left and saw Sam. Immediately Jimmy became defensive of his friend.

"He's not strange," said Jimmy. "And he happens to work for the Yankees."

"Yeah? What does he do?" asked Ricky.

"Well nothing. He used to work for the Yankees as an usher."

"Why doesn't he work for them anymore? He's retired" answered Jimmy.

Jimmy walked through the swinging gate door and headed over to see Sam in the stands. Sam smiled as he got closer.

"Hey, Sam! We won last Saturday," announced Jimmy.

"That's great. So you're in first place?" asked Sam.

"Yeah, but Community Bank is right behind us."

"Just keep playing hard. You can't do more than that. You had quite a week of practices."

"Yes," Jimmy said quietly. "Lou Gehrig! Can you believe that? It was just like I was there. It seemed so real!"

Sam smiled and looked up toward the field.

"Out there tonight, Jimmy, make it real for everyone to see," said Sam.

"I hope I can!" said Jimmy energetically.

"Remember what you've learned," stated Sam.

"Jimmy, let's go!" yelled Mr. Whitehill.

"I better get going," said Jimmy. "Oh, Mom and Dad will be here after Jillie finishes her new dance class. She wants to learn to dance like Shirley Temple."

Sam broke out laughing as Jimmy hustled onto the playing field.

The Eastside Service Station went down one, two, three in the top of the first. Jimmy fielded an easy chopper that was hit directly to him at second base.

In the bottom half of the inning, Joey Petruto lead off with a base hit up the middle. Bobby Sharples then pulled the ball into deep right field for a double. It was second and third, no outs, when Ricky hit a line drive into left that brought in one run. With first and third occupied, David Rockman was up. The first pitch was thrown way inside and hit David on the thigh. The umpire immediately yelled for David to take first base. David wasn't hurt, but he grumbled on his way to the bag.

Mike hit a slow bouncer to the shortstop. By the time the shortstop had fielded the ball, his only play was at first. He threw Mike out. Bobby Sharples scored, and the Sox were up 2 to 0.

Jimmy came to the plate ready to slam a line drive base hit for a couple of RBIs. He stepped into the batter's box, but then Mr. Whitehill called to the umpire for a time out. Mr. Whitehill ran down to Jimmy and said, "Give me one of those bunts you laid down during Sunday's practice."

"But Mr. Whitehill," said Jimmy, "with a base hit I might be able to bring in two runs."

"Let's play it safe with a bunt," said Mr. Whitehill. "Come on, you can do it."

Stepping up to the plate, Jimmy was trying to recall everything A1-33 had taught him during his bunting drill. The pitcher went to his wind up. Jimmy wanted everyone in the ballpark to know exactly what he was doing. He squared around, and the third and first baseman both came charging in.

The pitch was right down the middle. Jimmy moved the bat toward the ball and directed it to the left of the first baseman. He watched as contact was made, and the ball went right where his bat had commanded it to go. Jimmy started to run, looking only at first base. The ball passed the charging first baseman. Jimmy put on a burst of speed and touched the bag safely.

"Safe," called the umpire.

"Nice bunt!" yelled Mr. Roshay, who was coaching first.

As Jimmy walked back to the bag, Mr. Roshay continued talking to him.

"That was a sacrifice bunt turned into a clean hit with an RBI," Mr. Roshay said.

Jimmy stepped onto first base. It was his first hit of the year. His slump was over, and he did it with a bunt, just like Lou Gehrig had done in 1938.

Looking toward the stands, Jimmy saw Sam tip his hat in his usual way. Jimmy tipped his helmet back in return. It was an easy game for the Sox. The final score was 8 to 2.

Jimmy went 2-4 that game. His second time up, he hit a line drive to the third baseman for an out. A grounder back to the pitcher came on his third attempt. But Jimmy remembered what Lou Gehrig had told him, "you can't hit safely every time at bat." His last time up, Jimmy hit a sharp line drive into center field for a base hit.

CHAPTER 18

The team remained in first place with a 4 and 0 record. On the way to school, Jimmy and Ricky discussed the previous night's win against Eastside Service Station. Jimmy's batting average was now .143. He knew the bunt had helped him break his hitting slump. He was beginning to feel more confident.

"What are you doing after school?" Ricky asked Jimmy.

"Nothing. Why? What's going on?" asked Jimmy.

"There are new batting cages that opened up on Riverdale Avenue. How about we meet there at four and take some swings?"

"Sounds good."

The two friends turned and raced up the school's steps heading to class.

During recess, Jimmy went out into the schoolyard. A few guys were shooting basketballs. There was a pick-up game going on, and Jimmy sat in the stands watching with Joey Petruto. About five minutes before recess was over, Larry Barnes came walking across the basketball court. He was with a couple of other kids, mostly friends from his neighborhood.

Jimmy saw that Barnes had spotted him, and was walking toward him. Larry Barnes said something to one of his friends. Barnes then pointed to Jimmy, and the group started to laugh.

Joey looked up and saw Barnes heading his way. Larry Barnes and company approached Jimmy.

"McNeil, you're a pretty big guy with Rockman around," said Larry. "How tough are you now?"

"Get out of here, Barnes. No one's bothering you," Jimmy said sharply.

"You bother me, McNeil."

"That's your problem," Jimmy returned.

Barnes' face began to grow angry. He stepped on Jimmy's left foot, which was resting on the stands. Jimmy went to swipe Barnes's foot away when Larry grabbed him by the shoulders and pushed him backward. Jimmy felt his back hit the bleacher behind him. It hurt and Jimmy was beginning to feel nervous.

"Lay off, Larry!" Joey yelled.

"This has nothing to do with you, Petruto," said Larry. "Stay out of it."

"What's your problem Barnes," Jimmy asked again.

"I don't like twerps, and you're a twerp," announced Barnes.

"What you don't like is that we beat you opening day," said Jimmy.

"Wednesday night we play you again. We'll see how you do this time," said Barnes.

Just then the bell rang, and Barnes took his foot off of Jimmy's. He laughed and walked away with his friends.

Joey looked up at Jimmy and asked, "What's with him?"

"I don't know," returned Jimmy. "He's been acting like an idiot ever since we beat him opening day."

"Are you okay? He pushed you hard."

"Yeah, I'm fine. I'll get him back when we beat him next week."

Joey laid out the palm of his hand, and Jimmy slapped it to show his approval.

That afternoon, Jimmy met Ricky at the batting cages. As they were taking swings, Jimmy told Ricky what had happened during recess.

"Barnes can't stand to lose," Ricky said. "He thinks he's the world's greatest gift to sports. He thinks he's definitely going to become a professional ballplayer, and he'll never admit when he does something wrong. The two of you better learn to like each other, though."

"Why?" Jimmy asked.

"Because you'll both be on the All-Star team."

Jimmy laughed. "Did you notice my batting average is only .143? You can't make the All-Star team hitting like that."

"Jimmy, you've been so busy talking," said Ricky, "you haven't even noticed you just hit the last ten pitches into the back of the nets."

"You and Rockman will be the ones playing with Barnes, I'll be watching," said Jimmy.

"Maybe Barnes won't make the team if we knock him out of the box next week."

Jimmy smiled at Ricky's comment, and then slammed the ball into the deep left-hand corner of the batting cage.

On the way home, Jimmy was thinking about his run-in with Barnes. He was bothered by the way he had handled it. Jimmy thought that maybe he should have grabbed his foot and pushed him backward. It was eating away at him. He couldn't even concentrate on the next day's game.

When Jimmy entered his room that evening, he closed the door firmly behind him. The house seemed quiet. Jillie was already asleep, and his mom and dad were downstairs in the family room. Jimmy walked up to A1-33. He looked toward the stadium seat as if he was going to receive some magical answer as to how he should have handled Barnes.

"What would a professional baseball player do if he was being roused by another player? Would he get into a fight? What if that other player was stronger than he was?" Jimmy asked.

Jimmy didn't receive a response from A1-33. He shrugged his shoulders and climbed into bed.

It seemed like Jimmy laid in bed for hours before he could fall asleep. There was only one way he could feel better and that would be to confront Barnes. If he wants to fight, I'll fight him and get it over with, Jimmy thought. It was settled. Jimmy finally could feel himself getting tired, and he fell into a deep sleep.

CHAPTER 19

The next morning did not have the usual game day feeling for Jimmy. He had expected to dream about a way to confront Larry Barnes. Jimmy was disappointed he hadn't received any help from A1-33. The night before, Jimmy had decided today would be the day to handle Barnes. But he wasn't feeling confident about it. He wasn't even enthusiastic about playing in the game against Jean's Woodworks, which had a 2 and 2 record.

This was an important game. The Sox wanted to be undefeated when they played Community Bank on Wednesday evening. Jimmy went downstairs for breakfast.

"Are you okay?" Mom asked.

"Yeah, why?" asked Jimmy.

"Because you look pale and tired," Mom answered in a concerned tone.

"I'm all right."

"Well, sit down while I bring you something to eat."

Jimmy's mother placed breakfast in front of him and sat across from Jimmy with her cup of coffee.

"How's everything at school, Jimmy?" she asked.

"Fine," he answered.

Jimmy was hardly eating his food. He was just moving his fork around his plate.

"Excited about today's game?" Mom asked. "If you win, your team will be 5-0!"

"I know," Jimmy said flatly without even looking up.

He knew that mothers have a way of knowing when something is wrong. It's hard to hide things from them, he thought.

"Mom, everything's okay. I guess I'm just a little nervous," Jimmy said.

"Being nervous isn't bad. Sam told Dad and I that professional baseball players get nervous before games, just like kids do," stated Mom.

"Sam said that?" Jimmy asked.

"We talked about it on your opening day."

Jimmy half-smiled and got up from the table.

"Thanks, Mom. What time are you and Dad going to the field?' Jimmy asked.

"Oh, I forgot to tell you. Dad was called into work this morning; he may not be at today's game. Jillie and I will drive to the field at noon."

Disappointed with the news that his dad may not make it to the game, Jimmy cleared his barely eaten breakfast from the table. He thought how worried his mom would be if she knew it was Barnes who was making him nervous, and not today's game.

Jimmy arrived at the field in time for batting practice. Ricky joined him in the dugout while he was busily putting on his cleats.

"Going to go 4 for 4 today, Jimmy?" Ricky asked.

"I guess so," Jimmy responded.

"What do you mean you guess? You were slamming them in the cages yesterday. What's wrong with you? You look like you're about to get sick."

"I'm okay," Jimmy snapped.

"Forget I asked," Ricky said, as he ran out of the dugout and onto the field.

Jimmy followed and began warming up with the rest of the team. Mr. Whitehill crossed over the first base line on his way to the infield.

"Hey, Jimmy," he said cheerfully. "You hit the ball great last game."

"Thanks, Mr. Whitehill," Jimmy said with a smile.

"Keep it up. We need you on base more often.

While Jimmy continued to warm up, he looked over to the stands and saw Sam sitting with his mom and Jillie. Quickly, Jimmy left the playing field and trotted over to the fence.

"Hi, Sam!" yelled Jimmy.

Sam looked up, excused himself from Jimmy's mom and Jillie, and walked over to see him.

"Hi, Jimmy. Your mom tells me you're feeling nervous about today's game," Sam said. "There's nothing wrong with that, you know."

"I always get the jitters before a game, but that's not what I'm really nervous about," returned Jimmy.

"What's bothering you then?"

"Do you remember the pitcher from Community Bank, the team we played on opening day?"

"Larry Barnes?"

"Yeah. He and I don't exactly get along. Recently, he's been trying to push me around. Well, today I'm going to set him straight."

"How do you plan on doing that?"

"I'm going to stand up for myself and not let him get away with it."

"Jimmy, everyone must defend themselves," said Sam. "But I don't know if you're going about this in the right way. I think for now you should just ignore him."

"That's hard, Sam. I don't think it would work."

"He's probably just jealous you beat him on opening day. He'll get over it. In the meantime, you have a game that's ready to begin, and *that's* what you should be concentrating on."

Sam tipped his hat and turned away. Jimmy watched him walk back to the stands to rejoin his mom and Jillie.

"McNeil! Let's go! It's game time," yelled Mr. Whitehill.

Jimmy hustled into the dugout to hear his team's last instructions.

"This is a crucial game. Community Bank won last night and is now 4-1. We play them again Wednesday, and I want us to be up a game. We need today's win."

The Sox were charged up, and took an early lead. The Blue Sox were winning 3-0 in the bottom of the third. Jimmy grounded out to shortstop his first time up to bat. He was coming up to the plate now with Ricky on third and two outs. The count went to 2-0 and Jimmy began to maneuver his feet in the batter's box, concentrating on Lou Gehrig's instructions.

From behind the backstop, Jimmy suddenly heard, "Throw under hand to McNeil, and let's see if he can hit it."

Jimmy looked behind him and saw Barnes and his friends laughing. Jimmy turned back and looked at the pitcher. Jimmy was thinking about what Barnes was doing, and not the game. The pitch came in a little to the outside, and Jimmy swung anyway.

"Strike one," called the umpire.

"Way to swing, McNeil. Who taught you how to hit, some old man?" heckled Barnes.

Jimmy looked back at Barnes and gave him a long stare.

"Woo, I'm scared," Barnes shouted so everyone could hear.

That was it. Jimmy was going to knock this one out of the park just to show the big mouth. The next pitch was high. Jimmy knew it wasn't going to be in the strike zone, but he couldn't help himself. He swung and missed.

"Strike two," called the umpire.

Looking down, Jimmy couldn't believe he had just swung at that pitch.

"Settle down, Jimmy," called Mr. Whitehill. "You should've been on base with a walk by now!"

"Yeah, Jimmy. That's the only way you can get on," added Barnes.

The umpire stepped to the backstop and instructed Barnes and his buddies to sit in the stands quietly or leave the ballpark. He then returned to home plate and pointed to the pitcher, directing him to resume play.

The next pitch was right down the middle. Jimmy swung as if he was going for the fences. His bat got way out in front of the ball and he topped it. The ball bounced slowly to the second baseman for an easy third out. Despite all the noise on the field, the only thing Jimmy heard was the sound of Barnes' wicked laugh.

The Sox won the game 5-2, but Jimmy went 0 for 3 and only made one play at second base, which he bobbled before barely throwing the runner out. It was Barnes' fault, he thought to himself as he left the dugout.

Sam was waiting for Jimmy as he exited.

"Let's take a little walk while your mom pulls the car around," said Sam.

"Sam, I had a bad game, and it was all Barnes' fault," said Jimmy.

"No it wasn't," Sam interrupted. "It was your fault."

"How can you say that? Didn't you hear him making fun of me?"

"You let him," Sam said. "And you let him beat you today. You must learn to play the game that's on the field."

"That's what I was trying to do," Jimmy pleaded.

"It's a lesson you'll need to learn if you're ever going to make your dream come true. Your mom and Jillie are waiting for you. I'll see you Wednesday night when you play Community Bank."

Looking dejected, Jimmy quietly walked away. Deep inside, Jimmy knew Sam was right.

CHAPTER 20

Without even eating a bite of his food, Jimmy excused himself from the dinner table. He went to the family room and turned on the TV. As he sat down, his dad entered the room.

"Tough game today, son?"

Jimmy looked up and nodded his head in agreement.

"What's going on with you and Larry Barnes?" Dad asked.

"I don't know," said Jimmy. "Ever since the first game he's been looking to pick a fight."

"Jimmy, I don't want you to ever let anyone take advantage of you," said Dad sternly. "But, you must also have the discipline to conduct yourself in a proper manner."

"What do you mean? Let him make fun of me?"

"There are times when you must defend yourself, and there are times when you must be in control of yourself and your emotions."

Jimmy thought about this statement. It made sense, but he was still upset.

"All I know is that his big mouth affected my playing," said Jimmy with frustration. "I went 0 for 3, and I feel like I'm back in my batting slump."

"Listen, Jimmy. He only would've made you go 0 for 3 if he were pitching, and he wasn't," said Dad. "You need to take your mind off this kid."

"How do I do that?"

"Well, the Yankees are playing the Twins tonight on TV. Want to watch the game?"

Looking up at his dad with a smile, Jimmy agreed readily.

"Do you think Mom will make popcorn," asked Jimmy.

"I think Mom will probably be happy to see you eat anything. After all, you didn't touch your lasagna," answered Jimmy's father.

It was the bottom of the seventh, and the Yanks were down 4-1. Jimmy's mom and dad went upstairs leaving him alone to watch the game. Up at the plate for the Yankees was their lead off hitter. Jimmy could see the third baseman for the fielding team yelling at the batter as he was getting ready to hit. The Yankee hitter seemed bothered by what he was hearing and stepped out of the batter's box.

He then turned and began to walk up the third base line. Jimmy could see his jaw moving as he was yelling back to the third baseman. The umpire quickly called him back to home plate. The batter was visibly upset and seemed to be losing concentration. The pitcher fired a fastball and the Yankee hitter swung late and popped the ball straight back behind home plate. The catcher made an easy grab for the out.

The batter walked back toward the dugout in a huff, and Jimmy saw the third baseman laughing. The third baseman won the battle, Jimmy thought.

Suddenly, Jimmy found himself at Yankee Stadium, sitting in A1-33.

"How did I get here?" Jimmy asked in a confused voice.

"Calm down, Jimmy. You're here to learn," said A1-33. "That Yankee player had rabbit ears, you know."

"What are rabbit ears?"

"Rabbits get easily spooked by noises, and it throws them off their goal."

"I understand. But how can you avoid becoming bothered by someone who's yelling at you?"

"Just watch," said A1-33 pointing toward home plate. "You feel it's important to make a stand to maintain your pride. Look and watch who's at the plate right now."

Jimmy saw that Lou Gehrig was up. He thought it was strange that Lou Gehrig was playing with the present day Yankee team. Then Jimmy looked around and noticed that the billboard he had previously seen on TV had changed. Now it was advertising an old model car and a can of oil!

"Where are we?" Jimmy asked out loud.

"Yankee Stadium, 1937," answered A1-33. "Watch how your batting coach handles heckling."

"Are you kidding? Who would heckle Lou Gehrig?" Jimmy asked.

"Even the best get their share, Jimmy," said A1-33. "The difference is the way they deal with it. Now watch what makes Lou Gehrig a great athlete as well as a great person."

As Number Four stepped into the batter's box, a thunder of boos came from the fans at Yankee Stadium. Two rows in front of Jimmy, a man stood up and placed his hands around his mouth like a megaphone.

"Pull him out of there! He's a bum!" the man hollered.

"Hey, that's Lou Gehrig you're talking about!" Jimmy yelled back.

"Jimmy, no one can hear you," said A1-33 softly.

"I can hear them, and I don't like it!" Jimmy exclaimed.

"Lou could hear them also, if he wanted," A1-33 stated.

"How can he not listen to them? These aren't Yankee fans. Look at them screaming and waving their hands. Why are they doing that?"

"Lou struck out in the bottom of the 9th with the bases loaded and two outs against the Boston Red Sox yesterday. The fans are still upset about it. Just relax and watch what happens now."

The first pitch was high for ball one, and the crowd continued to heckle. Lou Gehrig didn't flinch a muscle. He just stayed in the batter's box, dug in, and waited for the next pitch.

How can he remain so calm, Jimmy wondered? The more the fans yelled, the greater his concentration became. The next pitch came in waist-high on the inside corner. Gehrig stepped forward opening up his hips while his body swung the bat around with the force of a helicopter propeller.

The ball flew right off the bat! The crowd silenced as everyone except Lou Gehrig watched the ball fly over the right field fence. Lou was already rounding first when the umpire waved his hand high in the air with a circular motion, indicating a home run.

The New York crowd quickly went from a hush to a roar of celebration, cheering their hero of the day. As Lou Gehrig touched second trotting toward third, his head turned toward the first base dugout and he looked up toward Jimmy. Their eyes locked. Lou Gehrig touched the tip of his cap and nodded his head. Jimmy slowly lifted his right hand and waved back to him.

The fans rose to their feet cheering.

"The fans sure changed their minds, huh?" Jimmy asked.

"That's right," said A1-33. "Lou Gehrig just concentrated on hitting the baseball, and didn't worry about the fans."

"How did he do it?"

"He didn't care that the fans were yelling names at him. He just blocked them out, and focused in on the pitcher, and then bang! So who do you think just had the last word?"

"Mr. Gehrig. He sure showed them."

"Did you learn something?" asked A1-33.

"I never should've let Barnes get to me at the plate," confessed Jimmy. "I was just like the Yankee who popped up in the game on TV. Barnes made a fool of me."

"Only because you let him," A1-33 added. "What did you notice about Gehrig?"

"He never broke his concentration."

"Yes. There are times when exercising self-control is more important than flexing your muscles, or as you and your friends say, mouthing off."

Jimmy smiled and nodded his head in agreement.

Then all of a sudden there was silence all around, and Jimmy was back in his family room. The TV was full of static, and the clock read three a.m. The nervous pit in his stomach had vanished. It had been replaced by hunger. Jimmy went into the kitchen to get something to eat, he then turned off the TV and walked upstairs. Jimmy entered his bedroom and smiled at A1-33.

"Thanks coach," he said out loud.

CHAPTER 21

It was Sunday afternoon, Jimmy decided to meet the guys over at the ballpark. They all wanted to watch the rained-out make-up game between Eastside Service Station and Jean's Woodworks. While riding his bicycle to Welty Park, Jimmy could feel the warmth of mid-spring.

Jimmy thought about all of the great things the summer would hold. No school, summer vacation, and hopefully, a spot on the traveling All-Star team!

He turned the corner. The ballpark was straight ahead. Behind the backstop he could see a crowd of people looking at something posted on the bulletin board. Ricky emerged from the crowd and went running over to Jimmy.

"They posted everyone's batting average," said Ricky. "David Rockman is leading the whole league!"

"Really?" Jimmy said with excitement. "Does he know it yet?"

"Yeah," Ricky replied. "He's over on the other side of the field with Joey and Mike. We were all waiting for you."

"How far down am I on the list?"

"Pretty far," Ricky said quietly. "Why don't you go check it out and meet us behind the center field fence."

"Sure," Jimmy replied dejectedly.

Jimmy parked his bicycle along the fence and pushed his way through the crowd that was reading the batting averages. When he got within viewing distance, he started at the top and began his way down the list. The top five names on the list read:

David Rockman, Blue Sox	.475
Larry Barnes, Community Bank	.455
Danny Gutin, Main Street	.395
José Sanchez, Community Bank	.385
Bobby Sharples, Blue Sox	.380

Jimmy was proud there were two members of the Blue Sox in the top five. There were also two Community Bank players, though. Jimmy worked his way down the list. Finally, number 68 out of 90 was Jimmy's name, with a batting average of .100.

"There's no way I'll make the All-Star team with an average like that. There's just no way," Jimmy said to himself.

Jimmy turned around, and much to his surprise, Sam was standing beside him.

"Hi Sam, what are you doing here?" Jimmy asked.

"I thought you might want to talk today," Sam answered.

"I know I can hit better than .100. I'm going to pick up that average and make the All-Star team," said Jimmy. "I want it badly, and I know I'm good enough to do it."

"You don't need any lessons from me today," said Sam. "You seem to have learned how to get your confidence back."

Looking up at Sam, Jimmy said, "I've had some great teachers."

Jimmy and Sam both smiled.

"Come on," Jimmy said. "Watch the game with us from behind the center field fence."

Sam agreed. Jimmy grabbed his bike, and they walked together slowly.

"Do you know about last night?" Jimmy asked.

"Yes," Sam replied.

"How does it happen?"

"You'll learn in good time."

When they were just about to meet up with the guys, Sam and Jimmy stopped talking. Jimmy knew this was a private conversation, and his friends wouldn't understand. Jimmy didn't even understand!

Ricky, Mike, David, and Joey were all there. Jimmy saw them looking at Sam. They had all seen him in the stands before, but had never met him.

"Hey, guys. This is Sam," announced Jimmy.

Jimmy made introductions one by one. They were all quiet, and Jimmy wasn't sure they appreciated him bringing an adult to watch the game with them. David Rockman was the last player introduced.

"You can really hit the baseball," Sam complimented. "Congratulations. You're leading the league."

David gave Sam a warm smile and said, "The season's not over. I hope I can keep it up."

"I'm sure you will. And just think, after baseball season, football will be here. You must be looking forward to that."

"I love football," said David. "It's my favorite sport!"

"Who's your favorite team?" Sam asked.

"The Giants, of course."

Sam began to tell David stories about football games he had watched while working at Yankee Stadium. The stadium had been used during the football season by the New York Giants, and had hosted National

Football League games for many years.

Next year, the Giants were moving to a stadium across the river in New Jersey. As Sam was telling his stories to David, Ricky jumped into the conversation.

"Hey, Sam! You ever been to a World Series game?" asked Ricky.

"Sure. The Yankees have played in more World Series games than any other team in the history of the game," Sam said.

Everyone became captivated by Sam's stories of Yankee Stadium. Before they knew it, they had missed the game between Eastside Service Station and Jean's Woodworks! Sam looked toward the field and said, "You have a big game this Wednesday night against Community Bank."

"We'll kill them!" Joey yelled.

"Just play hard," advised Sam.

"Are you going to be there Wednesday night?" David asked.

"If I can't watch the Yankees, I'm going to watch the Blue Sox," said Sam.

Jimmy and his teammates burst into a cheer of approval. As Sam was leaving, he said, "I'll see all of you Wednesday night."

Sam then tipped his hat and left.

"Man, he's a great guy. How'd you meet him?" Joey asked.

Mike answered: "Jimmy's father is on the work crew at Yankee Stadium, and that's how they became friends. Right, Jimmy?"

"Yeah, kind of," Jimmy answered hesitantly.

"Jimmy even has an old Yankee Stadium seat in his room that his dad gave him." Mike continued. "Don't you, Jimmy?"

But before Jimmy could answer, he heard a sneering voice behind him.

"You better get used to sitting in a stadium seat, McNeil," said Larry Barnes. "The way you play, you'll never get close to a major league field."

Jimmy looked directly into Larry Barnes' eyes and smiled. David Rockman stood up.

"I don't remember anyone inviting you into our conversation," said David.

"It's boring anyhow," said Larry backing up. "I'll see all you guys Wednesday night at the game. Hey, McNeil! Watch as your batting average drops even lower, if that's possible!"

As Larry Barnes walked away, Ricky and Jimmy said together, "What a jerk!"

The five members of the Blue Sox all started laughing and began talking again.

CHAPTER 22

The Blue Sox-Community Bank game was the talk of the school. Jimmy was walking to class when he heard his name called. He turned around and was glad to see David Rockman standing there.

"Hey, Jimmy," greeted David. "I'm ready for tonight's game. I wish it was game time right now!"

"I want Barnes to throw his best heat across the plate so I can smack one right over his head," Jimmy responded.

Rockman laughed, "I'll see you at the field."

Jimmy nodded and entered his classroom.

As he sat down, Jimmy recalled his latest lesson watching Lou Gehrig. He began to daydream, recalling every vision A1-33 had shown him.

"James, what is the square root of eighty-one?" asked Mrs. Rae. "Mr. McNeil, are you paying attention?"

"No. I mean, yes, Mrs. Rae," Jimmy said nervously.

Everyone in the class started laughing.

"Well, what is the answer then?" asked Mrs. Rae again.

"Answer to what?" Jimmy asked.

His teacher's face turned stone cold. He began to sink in his chair as she lowered her face closer to his.

"James, you and I are going to meet after school today," she said sternly. "If you want to get lost daydreaming during my class, then you can make it up after three o'clock."

Oh no! Not today, Jimmy thought to himself. He slouched in his seat, and felt the stares of all his classmates shooting through him.

When his math class had finished, Jimmy stopped at Mrs. Rae's desk. He decided he would try to plea for a release from his punishment.

"I'm really sorry I wasn't paying attention," said Jimmy. "I won't let it happen again."

"I know you won't, James," she said, staring at the work in front of her.

"Well, is it okay if I make up the class time tomorrow?"

"No, James," she snapped. "Why not today?"

"Well, we have a big game tonight and I really . . ."

"You'll be home in plenty of time for your game," Mrs. Rae interrupted. "I had a similar problem today with a student named Larry Barnes. He wasn't paying attention either. Apparently he also has a big game tonight, which he also thought was more important than class."

Jimmy felt his heart drop. He knew what Mrs. Rae was going to say next.

"The two of you can enjoy each other's company today," she said coldly.

At precisely 3:05, Jimmy entered the classroom for detention. Mrs. Rae quickly entered the room.

"Take a seat, Mr. McNeil, while I provide you with a little work, hopefully this will prove more interesting, or at least more important, to you."

Mrs. Rae brought over three pages of square roots, and instructed Jimmy to calculate them. This will take an hour, Jimmy thought to himself. That brings the time to 4:06. Then I'll need another twenty minutes to get home. And then . . .

Mrs. Rae hollered out, "Start your calculations. And when Mr. Barnes decides to arrive, he can join you as well."

Jimmy finished the detention work in approximately half an hour. He stayed completely focused, as he wanted to finish quickly. He didn't even notice that Barnes hadn't shown up. He handed the work to Mrs. Rae, who quickly reviewed his effort. He watched as she made three strokes with her infamous red pen. She then looked up at him and smiled.

"Very good, James. You didn't need detention to learn your work," said the teacher. "Now just do what you're supposed to in class, and realize that your ball games are extra-curricular activities. When you become a high school and college athlete, you'll need to always keep your grades up. School is very important, Jimmy. It should never be overlooked. Do you understand me?"

Jimmy couldn't believe Mrs. Rae had said all that in one breath.

"Yes, Mrs. Rae. I do understand," said Jimmy politely and sincerely.

"Then you may go," she said.

Jimmy thanked her, and immediately began running home to prepare for the big game.

CHAPTER 23

It was almost game time and you could just feel the energy at Welty Park. Cars were beginning to pull into the parking lot, and it seemed like every player in the league was showing up to see the game. By the end of the night, the Sox could have sole possession of first place, with a two game lead. Or, they could be tied dead even for first place with Community Bank.

The first-string pitchers for both teams were on the mound for the game: Bobby Sharples for the Blue Sox and, of course, Larry Barnes for Community Bank.

Jimmy entered the field's gate and quickly began to loosen up with Joey Petruto.

"Hey, Jimmy! I heard you got detention with Barnes today from old lady Rae," said Joey.

"Yeah, can you believe it?" asked Jimmy. "She kept me after school for not paying attention."

"How was it spending detention with Barnes? Did he mouth off?"

"He didn't even show up." Jimmy said as they continued to throw.

"He didn't show up?" asked Joey. "That guy is dead meat with the old lady. What'd she say?"

"Nothing. I just minded my own business."

Joey smiled. "That's a good idea."

The team ended its pre-game warm up, and Mr. Whitehill called everyone into the dugout.

"Okay, everyone. This is a grudge match for Community Bank," said Mr. Whitehill. "We're the only team that has beaten them so far. They want to win this game badly."

"Not as bad as us!" Jimmy blurted out.

Mr. Whitehill looked over to Jimmy and held his fist up in the air. Grinning, he shook it in an approving manner.

"That's right. Now let's go hard tonight, team," yelled Mr. Whitehill. "We want first place all to ourselves!"

The Blue Sox joined in with a loud cheer.

The Sox were the home team this evening. The starting players were standing by the dugout fence waiting for the umpire to indicate it was game time so they could take the field. David Rockman tapped Jimmy on the arm with his glove.

"Look who's over there," David said pointing.

Jimmy looked right, and there, leaning on the first base line fence, was Sam. He was looking right into the dugout. Sam smiled at Jimmy and tipped his hat. The Sox took the field and the game was ready to begin.

Bobby Sharples threw six warm-up pitches, and then the team tossed the ball around the infield. Community Bank's lead off hitter was José Sanchez.

Jimmy quickly recalled the opening game when José had hit the ball between David and himself. Jimmy took two steps over to his left. David looked at Jimmy showing that he had remembered as well. Their entire team filled the ballpark with encouraging chatter.

"Come on, Bobby," yelled Jimmy.

Sharples delivered the first pitch. José swung and missed for strike one. Sharples chucked the second pitch on the inside corner for a called strike two.

Joey Petruto yelled, "One more Bobby, you can do it!"

Bobby threw a fastball right down the middle. José didn't even see it.

"Strike three!" yelled the umpire.

The Blue Sox all cheered and Mr. Whitehill nodded his head to congratulate Bobby.

The second batter hit a bouncing ball back to Bobby on the mound. He easily handled it and threw to Rockman at first for out number two. Slowly walking up to the plate came Larry Barnes. The entire infield turned to the outfield and directed them to take a couple of steps back.

The count on Barnes quickly went to 1-1. Bobby Sharples wound up and threw his third pitch. Barnes opened up his swing and slammed the ball deep into left field. Jimmy had a bad feeling about the ball the moment he saw it leave the bat. Soon Larry Barnes was trotting around the bases. The ump waved his hand to show it was a home run. Jimmy walked over to his team's pitcher.

"I can't stand that guy," said Bobby.

"It's still early," said Jimmy. "Shake it off."

Bobby set himself on the mound and threw his next pitch to Community Bank's clean-up hitter. The batter swung and hit a low bouncing ground ball heading Jimmy's way. Jimmy crouched down low and moved in on the ball. His glove scooped it off the ground. Jimmy then positioned himself and threw to David at first for the third out.

Mr. Whitehill encouraged the team as they entered the dugout.

"Let's go get them," shouted the manager. "Petruto, Sharples, and Birk, let's make something happen!"

Barnes began warming up on the mound. His pitches echoed through the park as they hit the catcher's glove.

Joey was a great lead off hitter, but against Barnes he went down swinging on three straight fastballs. Sharples and Birk didn't do any better and the inning soon was over. The entire team became quiet. Mr. Whitehill started cheering from the dugout.

"Let's go team," he hollered. "We still have five innings of ball left!"

The team hustled out to the field. Bobby pitched a great half-inning and soon the Sox were up again.

As David Rockman, the league's leading hitter, approached the batter's box, Jimmy looked to his right and saw Sam standing by the fence. Jimmy walked over to talk to him.

"Hi Sam," said Jimmy.

"Jimmy, I want you to concentrate on everything you've learned so far," said Sam. "Barnes's fastball is coming right down the middle. Watch one closely so you can set your timing. You can do it, I know you can!"

"I know it too," said Jimmy. "I really feel I can."

The count went to 1-2 on Rockman. Barnes delivered his next pitch and Rockman cracked a line drive into the left center field gap. David rounded first and easily went to second base for a double. Mike Laffey began his walk toward home plate, and Jimmy took his place in the on-deck circle.

Mr. Whitehill met Mike at home plate and said something to him. Jimmy soon realized he had given Mike the signal to bunt. Mike squared around to bunt on the first pitch, the ball popped up to catcher. Mike shook his head as he passed Jimmy on the way to the dugout.

"He's tough to hit today, Jimmy," said Mike frowning.

Jimmy slowly approached the batter's box, and looked toward the mound. Barnes stood there grinning. Beyond the mound Jimmy saw David Rockman standing on second base clapping his hands in encouragement. Before Jimmy had completely entered the batter's box, he looked toward Mr. Whitehill, who signaled him to swing away. Jimmy stepped up to the plate.

All of a sudden a vision of Lou Gehrig flashed through Jimmy's mind. He was now ready to use everything he learned. Jimmy made his stance comfortable, gripped the bat, and prepared himself for a Barnes fastball.

Barnes tried to stare Jimmy down, but Jimmy didn't get upset. Instead, he just prepared for the pitch. Barnes wound up, kicked high toward home plate, and threw a fastball straight down the middle. Watching the pitch, Jimmy's eyes timed the ball and his mind calculated when it would be the right time to swing.

"Strike one," yelled the umpire.

The catcher quickly called out to Barnes, "He didn't even see it! Throw the same one."

Jimmy collected himself in the batter's box and waited for the next pitch. He could hear noise coming from everywhere, but Jimmy just tuned out the chatter. His full concentration was focused on hitting the ball. Barnes began his wind up.

Jimmy's hands re-gripped the handle of the bat. He watched the ball leave Barnes' hand. Jimmy timed his swing perfectly and he met the ball right on the meat of the bat, sending a powerful line drive back up the pitcher's mound.

Barnes saw the ball coming and ducked as it went over his head and into center field. Rockman was running hard, and Mr. Whitehill waved him around, indicating he should run home. The center fielder threw the ball wide to the left of the catcher and it rolled past the backstop. Jimmy scooted into second and waved at Rockman as he headed toward the dugout.

Jimmy stood proudly on second base, knowing he had just knocked in a run to tie the ball game. He looked toward the stands and saw everyone cheering. For the time being, Barnes was quiet. There was still one out, and Stanley Johnson came up to the plate for the Sox.

Jimmy knew Stanley's batting average was a little lower than his own, and figured that Mr. Whitehill might flash him the bunt signal. Jimmy prepared himself to run to third base if Stanley laid down a sacrifice bunt.

Barnes went into his wind up, Stanley squared around and properly pushed his bat forward, directing a beautiful bunt down the third base line. Community Bank's third baseman, Barnes, and the catcher, all charged the ball.

José Sanchez, the third baseman, came up with the ball. He initially turned to throw Jimmy out at third, but nobody was covering the bag. He then whirled around and threw wildly to first in an attempt to get Johnson. The ball was thrown over the first baseman's head and out of the playing field. Jimmy had already reached third and was rounding the base to head home. The umpire directed him in to score. He then motioned for Johnson to advance to second base.

Jimmy rushed to greet his cheering team in the dugout.

"You sure showed Barnes! Way to go!" Joey yelled.

"Hey, guys. It's only 2 to 1. We need a couple more," Mr. Roshay said.

The entire team was brought back to reality in an instant. After all, it was only the bottom of the second inning.

The next two batters for the Blue Sox struck out and Barnes showed he was beginning to gain momentum again. From the third inning on the game moved quickly. It was definitely a pitchers duel between Sharples and Barnes.

In the top of the fourth, Barnes led off with a double for Community Bank. The next batter drove him in with a well-hit ball, and all of a sudden the game was tied 2-2. Going into the bottom of the inning, the Blue Sox knew they needed another run.

"Mike, Jimmy, Stanley. Come over here," called Mr. Whitehill.

The three boys huddled around their manager listening intently.

"Mike, I want you to wait for the right pitch and bunt it down the first base line," said Mr. Whitehill. "Community Bank seems to get confused covering bases. Jimmy, is your bat still feeling pretty hot?"

"Yes sir, Mr. Whitehill," said Jimmy.

"Good. I want you swinging away. Stanley, let's see you lay down another bunt just like before. We need to make their infield do a little work. Does everyone understand?"

"Yes sir," answered the ballplayers together.

Mike Laffey took his spot at home plate as Jimmy stepped into the on-deck circle. Barnes delivered his first pitch to Mike, which made Mike jump back from the plate. It was an inside fastball for ball one. On the next pitch, Barnes went inside again, this time hitting Mike square on the upper arm. Mike yelled out in pain, and Mr. Whitehill and the umpire quickly surrounded Mike to see if he was okay.

Mike rubbed his arm while his face grimaced. Just looking at Mike, Jimmy could see how much pain he was experiencing. Holding his arm, Mike started his trot down to first base. The entire ballpark, including both dugouts, started to cheer for him.

Jimmy looked at Mike rubbing his arm on first base. Jimmy became determined to knock Mike around. He entered the batter's box and waited to see if Barnes was going to try any of his wise-guy moves. Barnes's face became stern, and Jimmy could see the determination in his eyes.

The first pitch was thrown outside for ball one. Jimmy wondered if Barnes was beginning to lose control. Barnes wound up and fell off the mound on his next pitch. From the time the ball left his hand, Jimmy could see it would not even be close to the plate. The ball went low and outside and skidded past the catcher. Mike darted from first to second.

The count went to 2-0. Community Bank's manager, Mr. Harrison, called time out. He slowly walked out to the mound to speak with Larry Barnes who was upset and grumbling. Barnes looked down at the ground as his manager spoke with him. How can he learn from his coach if he doesn't ever look at him or pay attention? Jimmy wondered.

During the time out, Mr. Whitehill walked over to speak with Jimmy.

"Barnes is having a hard time," said the manager. "Continue taking pitches until he throws a strike."

"Sure thing, Mr. Whitehill," said Jimmy.

The umpire yelled out to the mound, "Let's go! We have a game to finish."

Community Bank's manager ran back to his dugout. Barnes stepped onto the rubber. Jimmy positioned himself in the box and watched as Barnes threw ball three. With three balls and no strikes, Jimmy definitely wouldn't be swinging on the next pitch.

Barnes stared at the catcher and fired a pitch right down the middle for a called strike one. As the ball passed him, Jimmy mentally timed it as if he were going to swing. Now I know what to do, he thought.

"Okay, Jimmy! It's got to be a good one," encouraged Mr. Whitehill.

"Come on Jimmy! Bring me in," Mike called from second.

Barnes again stepped onto the rubber. Jimmy dug his back foot secure in the dirt, held the bat off his shoulder, and clearly watched the next fastball coming his way. Jimmy stepped forward. His swing sent a line drive deep down the left field line, and he took off quickly for first base. Heading toward third, Mike was waved home by Mr. Whitehill.

The ball landed fair by two feet and started to bounce toward the left field fence. Mike scored easily, and Jimmy went to second with a stand up double and another RBI.

The crowd was cheering as the Blue Sox regained the lead. Barnes was on the mound hanging his head. He took the ball and banged it hard into his glove before stepping back onto the rubber.

No one could tell what came over Larry Barnes, but he threw nine straight strikes. Johnson, Reynolds, and Paeper all went down one, two, and three. Jimmy was stranded on second to end the fourth inning.

In the fifth, the pitching battle continued as Sharples and Barnes each retired their first three batters. The Sox took the field in the top of the sixth. If they could hold Community Bank scoreless for three more outs, they would secure a two game lead for first place.

The number nine batter led off for Community Bank, and quickly popped up to Jimmy, who made the play easily. José Sanchez drilled a ball into deep left field and with his speed, turned the play into a triple. The next batter was walked and all of a sudden, Larry Barnes stepped up to the plate again.

Mr. Whitehill called time out and walked toward the mound. He had a brief meeting with Bobby and Mike, and then headed back to the dugout. Before Sharples threw his next pitch, Mike extended his right arm out, signaling for an intentional walk. The Community Bank dugout and fans began booing.

"Chicken," yelled one of the player's fathers.

"Let the kids play ball," yelled another player's mother.

Jimmy knew it was good baseball strategy. Barnes was capable of hitting one out at any time. After four pitches, Barnes trotted down to first. The bases were now loaded with one out. The infielders all backed up to prepare for a double play. Bobby threw his first pitch. The hitter swung and sent a pop up straight into the air.

"Infield fly rule, the batter is out," yelled the umpire.

There were now two outs with the bases loaded. Alyssa Monagle stepped up to the plate for Community Bank. Bobby wound up and delivered his pitch. Alyssa hit a bouncing ball to Ricky at shortstop. Jimmy moved toward second base to cover the bag for the game winning force out. Ricky was sitting back waiting for the ball. When it finally got to him, he bent down and went to grab the ball. Ricky missed the ball, though, and it rolled into the outfield.

Ricky slammed his glove down on the ground in frustration but Jimmy knew the play was far from over. He ran out to shallow left field to retrieve the ball. By the time he got to it, two runs had scored. Barnes was trying to stretch his way to third. Jimmy fired the ball to Joey Petruto, who laid down the tag.

"Out!" yelled the ump.

It was the final out of the inning, but the damage had been done. Community Bank had scored two runs to take the lead going into the bottom of the sixth.

"Let's go, let's go," encouraged Mr. Whitehill. "Come on! We still have last licks in this game. It's Rockman, Laffey, and McNeil. I know you can do it."

Rockman came to bat and crushed the ball on Barnes's second pitch. The outfielders were playing back, and the left fielder came up with the catch. Laffey struck out, and McNeil came to the plate with two outs. Shaking off the pressure, Jimmy delivered a single between the shortstop and the third basemen.

With two outs and one runner on, Stanley Johnson popped up to the pitcher. Community Bank won the game and Barnes leaped off the mound with his arms held high and the ball in his right hand.

Jimmy felt the first baseman streak by him as Community Bank's entire team ended up on the infield grass. They were cheering and celebrating like they had just won the World Series. Jimmy felt a strange feeling in his stomach. It was his first loss of the season and he didn't like how it felt.

Mr. Whitehill gathered the team together, and Stanley Johnson was the last one to walk into a very quiet dugout. Mr. Whitehill spoke slowly. At first, he sounded disappointed. But as he continued to speak, his words became encouraging.

"It's okay," Mr. Whitehill said. "Going undefeated is a very difficult thing to do. This will just make us work that much harder!"

"We wouldn't have lost the game if I hadn't missed the ground ball," interrupted Ricky.

"No way," said Rockman. "If I had gotten on base, McNeil would've knocked me in."

"Hold on," said Mr. Whitehill. "This was a good game, and a game doesn't depend upon one single play. But do you hear yourselves? You're all trying to accept responsibility for the game."

Everyone on the team looked around at everyone else.

"The Blue Sox is a team, a real team, and I'm proud of you," said the manager with enthusiasm. "This is just the type of attitude that'll pick you up and bring the team together. We'll win the next game and then go on and grab the pennant. Now go home and get some rest. I'll see you all Saturday at noon."

One by one, the team started to pile out of the dugout.

"McNeil," called Mr. Whitehill. "Wait a second!"

Jimmy stayed back as the rest of the team left.

"You played a great game today," Mr. Whitehill said. "You're hitting was great. I think you're really coming along as a complete ballplayer."

"Thanks, Mr. Whitehill," Jimmy said before turning around and leaving.

Jimmy's mom, dad, Jillie, and Sam were all waiting for him.

"Great game!" said Dad.

"But we lost," said Jimmy.

"Not by much," added Mom.

Sam then joined the conversation, "Jimmy, there never was a Yankee team that went undefeated. You have nothing to be ashamed of. Do you know you improved your batting average to .307 with your hitting today?"

"How do you know that?" Jimmy asked.

"When you've watched as much baseball as I have, you learn to calculate batting averages quickly," said Sam.

"Sam, you're probably the greatest baseball fan I've ever known," said Dad.

The family laughed, but everyone agreed. Sam was a great baseball fan.

"Thanks, Mac, but over the years I've watched ballgames with fans even better than I," Sam said.

As they left the ballpark, Jimmy noticed that Barnes was on his bicycle, heading home by himself. Jimmy was surprised Barnes was alone. Maybe that's why he shows off so much, Jimmy thought. For the first time in his life, Jimmy felt bad for Larry Barnes. Larry had no one to share his success with.

Jimmy looked at his family, and then at Sam. He realized how lucky he was to have their support.

Jimmy knew he would never let Barnes bother him again. After going three for three against him, he had the confidence to face any pitcher in the league.

CHAPTER 24

A manager has his cards dealt to him and he must play them.

–Miller Huggins

As the weeks rolled on, Jimmy and his team racked up the wins. After their loss to Community Bank, they won eight straight games. The Blue Sox team record went to 13-1. Although their record was great, they had only secured a tie for first place, since Community Bank had also won the rest of their games!

The last scheduled game of the season was on Sunday. The League Championship would be decided in the final bout between the Blue Sox and Community Bank.

In the last eight games, Jimmy's batting average had improved dramatically, moving up to .375. He was now the third leading batter in the league, behind Barnes, who was batting .385, and David Rockman, who was batting a whopping .450.

Mr. Whitehill said that whatever his mom was feeding him for dinner, he wanted her to feed it to the entire team. Jimmy wondered if everyone would enjoy peanut butter sandwiches and two glasses of orange juice, because that's what his mom gave him before each and every game.

Mr. Whitehill called an evening practice. It was Friday, and with only two days left before the regular season's biggest game, he wanted to be sure the Blue Sox were ready. Jimmy was pedaling his bike to Ricky's house. He skidded to a stop and then went up and knocked on the door. Mrs. Birk answered.

"Hi, Mrs. Birk," Jimmy said politely.

"Hello, Jimmy," said Mrs. Birk. "Are you here to see Ricky?"

"Well, we have a practice tonight at Welty Park, and I thought we'd go over together."

"Oh. Well, Ricky can't go to practice tonight," said Mrs. Birk. "He received notification from school today that he's failing history and science."

As the words came out of Mrs. Birk's mouth, Jimmy viewed Ricky slowly walking down the stairs. Ricky lifted his hand and slightly waved to Jimmy. Jimmy lifted his eyebrows, trying to ask Ricky what was going on without speaking. Ricky shrugged his shoulders and frowned.

"Jimmy, would you do me a favor?" asked Mrs. Birk.

"Sure," Jimmy said softly.

"Please tell Mr. Whitehill that Ricky will not be playing in Sunday's game."

"What? Mrs. Birk, Sunday's game is for the league championship! Ricky has to be there!" exclaimed Jimmy.

"No, Jimmy. Ricky is going to be home studying," said Mrs. Birk. "School ends next week. If Ricky doesn't want to end up in summer school, he needs to pass his remaining exams."

Mrs. Birk wished Jimmy goodnight and closed the door. Jimmy rode his bike to the field. All the way to practice, he couldn't help but worry. The Blue Sox wouldn't have their shortstop and number three hitter for the championship game!

Jimmy stopped by the first base dugout where Mr. Whitehill and the team were gathering. He let the bike slide out from underneath him, and it crashed against the fence along the first base line.

"Hey, slow down," exclaimed Mr. Whitehill. "What's the panic? I know you like to be on time, but practice hasn't even started yet."

Trying to catch his breath, Jimmy blurted out, "I just came from Ricky Birk's house."

"Is everything okay with Ricky? What's the matter?" asked Mr. Whitehill concerned.

"Ricky's failing two classes," said Jimmy, "and his mother said he has to study on Sunday and can't play against Community Bank."

"No way," Mike cried out.

"Come on, that's not fair," Joey added.

"Hold on guys," said Mr. Whitehill. "This is Mrs. Birk's choice. If she feels Ricky has let his studies go, then it's her decision as a parent."

Everyone was quiet. The boys were thinking over what Mr. Whitehill had said. It made sense, but they still really wanted Ricky to play.

"But Mr. Whitehill, Sunday's game means the pennant," said Jimmy.

"Yes," said Mr. Whitehill, "and baseball is still a team sport. There are other members of the team that'll have to fill the position."

"But who will play shortstop?" Jimmy asked in a panic.

"You will, Jimmy," said Mr. Whitehill calmly. "Now I want everyone to take the field. Let's go!"

The Blue Sox hustled onto the field, and this time Jimmy headed straight to shortstop. Mr. Whitehill placed Stanley Johnson at second base.

Everyone was quiet during practice, and Jimmy could tell Mr. Whitehill was getting frustrated with the team. After the batting drill was over, he called everyone into the dugout. They all took their usual places on the bench, and Mr. Whitehill slowly began to pace back and forth.

"How many of you like to watch professional sports?" their manager asked.

Everyone raised their hand.

"How about football?" Mr. Whitehill asked. "Anyone follow the Jets or the Giants?"

"I do," David yelled with zeal.

"Okay David, now what happens when a player gets taken out of a game because of an injury?"

"Another one takes his place," answered David.

"And how does the rest of the team treat him when he comes on the field?"

"Well, Mr. Whitehill, they jump up and down and get all pumped up and ready to make the next play."

Mr. Whitehill nodded his head and stopped his pacing. He stood still and looked at everybody on the team intensely.

"Do you see them bow their heads and give up?" Mr. Whitehill asked.

"No way!" exclaimed David. "Pro players don't give up."

"Then why are all of you?" Mr. Whitehill asked. "This entire team has played too hard all season to give up now because one player can't make it to the game. What type of sport is this?"

"A team sport," they all yelled.

"And are we a team?" asked the manager.

"Yes!" they all yelled back.

"Then Sunday, when we win the pennant," said Mr. Whitehill raising his voice. "We'll win it because we're a team!"

Mr. Whitehill's speech had really affected Jimmy, and he could tell it had also affected everyone else on the team. Mr. Whitehill told his players to head home and be at the ballpark at noon on Sunday. As Jimmy began to walk away, Mr. Whitehill called him over.

Mr. Whitehill took off his baseball hat, ran his fingers through his hair, and put his hat back on. Jimmy wondered if he had done something wrong and was going to get a lecture. He began to feel nervous.

"You know, Jimmy, you've had a great season," began Mr. Whitehill. "Your batting average is one of the best in the league, and you're the best infielder I've ever coached."

Jimmy was definitely starting to feel better. He leaned forward to show his manager he was really listening.

"I should've moved you to shortstop earlier in the year, but we were winning and I didn't want to change the lineup," said Mr. Whitehill. "Now it has to be changed, and I know you're the right one for the position."

Jimmy didn't respond. He just listened.

"I also should've moved you up in the batter's lineup recently, but I didn't," continued the manager. "Now you'll have to move to the number three spot. You should have no problem making the All-Star team. If we win on Sunday, I'll manage the team this summer, and you'll be my starting shortstop. I know you can do it."

"I won't let you down, Mr. Whitehill," Jimmy said seriously.

"I know you won't, but promise me one thing."

"Sure."

"Please have a peanut butter sandwich and two glasses of orange juice before the game on Sunday."

"Are you kidding? My mother wouldn't let me out of the house without it!"

Mr. Whitehill grinned and Jimmy left the dugout. He lifted his bicycle off the ground. On the way home, he wasn't even excited about what Mr. Whitehill had told him. He felt bad for Ricky, and thought he was taking his friend's position. Ricky was one of his best friends, and he hoped he wouldn't be hurt or angry.

CHAPTER 25

The McNeils spent the next day together as a family. First, they went to the Cross County Mall to get Jillie a new bathing suit. Then, Dad went to the hardware store to buy supplies for a new cabinet he was building.

In the car, Jillie asked where they would be going for summer vacation.

"Are we going to the beach again?" asked Jillie.

"Would you like to go there again?" Mom asked.

"Oh yeah, I love the beach," said Jillie with excitement.

"But we go there every year," said Jimmy flatly. "Can we go somewhere different this year?"

Jimmy's father looked over at his wife sitting in the passenger seat. Mom turned around so that she was facing the kids in the backseat.

"Where would you like to go?" Mom asked.

"I don't know. How about Cooperstown and the Baseball Hall of Fame?" Jimmy asked back.

"I don't want to go there," Jillie whined. "I watch your stupid baseball games every week. I want to go somewhere fun."

"Jillie's right," said Mom. "It's a family vacation, and we do see plenty of baseball during the spring."

"Yeah," Jillie said. "I'm glad that tomorrow's your last game."

Jimmy crossed his arms. He was upset. He wanted to go to the Baseball Hall of Fame. He was tired of going to the beach every year.

"You know, Jimmy. Tomorrow might not be your last game," Dad said.

"That's right," Mom added. "It seems like you have a really great chance of making the All-Star team, Jimmy."

"What All-Star team? What are you all talking about?" asked Jillie.

Dad explained what the All-Star team was to Jillie. She frowned and began to fidget in the backseat.

"Stop moving around so much," Jimmy yelled at her. "Can't you stay still?"

"Why don't you try and make me," she snapped back.

Jimmy and Jillie continued to bicker. Mom turned around and told them both that if she heard any more out of the backseat, there would be no vacation at all this year. They both became quiet, but Jillie continued to make faces at her brother. Soon the family had arrived at the hardware store.

"Do you remember the book I received about Cooperstown for Christmas?" Jimmy asked his father as they walked inside the store.

"Yes, Jimmy," answered Dad with a hesitant tone in his voice.

"Well, I read in the book that Cooperstown is right near Lake Ostego."

"What are you getting at, Jimmy?"

"Well at that lake, there's swimming and boating and all sorts of fun stuff.

"Is that so," his father returned. "Well, maybe we can look into that Jimmy."

"And of course there's the Baseball Hall of Fame," Jimmy added, "which is a historical library and museum. I would consider it very educational."

"Okay, Jimmy. Don't lay it on too thick, son."

That evening, during the family dinner, Jimmy started really worrying about the Championship Game for the first time. He hadn't felt butterflies this bad since opening game! Different scenarios ran all through his mind. What if I make an error at shortstop and let a run in, he thought. Or worse, what if I strike out against Barnes with a runner in scoring position?

Jimmy lost his appetite and he could tell his mother knew exactly what was on his mind. She took his half-finished plate away without saying a word.

Jimmy quietly left the table and walked into the living room. He was sitting down on the couch in front of the TV when his mom entered the room.

"Jimmy, where's your book on Cooperstown?" his mother asked.

"It's in my room," Jimmy replied.

"Go get it. I'd like to take a look at the family vacation spots you've been talking about."

Jimmy quickly ran up the stairs, turned the corner, and entered his bedroom. He came to a screeching stop at the bookshelf. Jimmy's fingers rapidly ran across the books, looking for the Cooperstown book. Finally, his right hand grabbed it and pulled it off the shelf. It was a large book with mostly pictures.

With the book tucked under his arm, Jimmy looked down at A1-33.

Mom wants to see about Cooperstown," explained Jimmy to the box seat. "I'll see you later."

When Jimmy arrived in the living room, Mom was waiting patiently for him. She reached out for the book. Jimmy was excited about the idea of going to Cooperstown during the summer, and he seemed to forget all about the Championship Game.

"Well, where are all the fun family activities that you told us about?" asked Mom.

"Right here," Jimmy said, turning the pages. "See, here's the Hall of Fame Baseball Museum. And here's the ballpark!"

"This is great, Jimmy. This would certainly keep us busy," said Mom. "But what about your sister?"

"Hold on. I'm getting there!"

Jimmy continued to turn the pages, until he saw a picture of Lake Ostego. In the picture were all types of boats, roped off swimming areas, and families having picnics on the shore. Surrounding the lake were nice looking hotels, many of them with swimming pools and some with playgrounds. Jimmy could see his mother studying the picture and nodding her head with approval.

"There's more, Mom," Jimmy said. "Look at this next page."

Mom continued to look through the book. She smiled as she turned each page. Jimmy closed the book and called Jillie into the room.

"Do you remember the commercial you saw on TV last year with Little Bo Peep?" Mom asked.

"The one where she was walking around wearing a pretty dress and looking for her sheep?" Jillie asked.

"Yes. How would you like to go there this summer?"

"I'd love to, Mom!"

"That's great, because Story Book Village is only twenty-five miles from Cooperstown!"

Jimmy's mother smiled, and proceeded to explain to her two children all about Story Book Village. Jimmy didn't seem very excited, and Mom looked over at him.

"Jimmy, if Jillie can go to a baseball museum, you can certainly go to Story Book Village," Mom said.

"You're right, Mom," Jimmy said softly.

Jimmy knew his mother had put him in his place. If he had any chance of visiting Cooperstown this summer, he'd better agree to go and see Little Bo Peep.

"What's going on? Where are we going?" Dad asked as he walked in.

Mom asked everyone to sit down, and the family gathered to plan out the vacation. It was a great evening overall, and everyone was excited about making plans for the summer. There was something for everybody in Cooperstown. The only thing they couldn't decide on was when they would go. If Jimmy made the All-Star team, hopefully he would be playing for most of the summer.

It was getting late, and Jimmy and Jillie were encouraged to go to sleep. Jimmy had felt a big punch to his stomach after his dad started talking about baseball again. The thought of the pennant-winning game made him really nervous. He didn't think he'd ever be able to sleep as he crawled into bed. He wasn't feeling confident about playing shortstop. Jimmy turned his head on his pillow and looked toward his box seat.

Suddenly, a bright light flashed from the seat's brass number. Jimmy rubbed his eyes, and when he opened them, he found himself in Yankee Stadium. He was standing in front of A1-33. Fans were beginning to enter the stadium, and the ground crew was still working on the field. Jimmy could tell that it was game day.

Instinctively, Jimmy looked toward familiar sections of Yankee Stadium to see if he could determine the approximate year and era of the Yankees he was visiting. In straightaway center field, the Yankee monuments were on the warning track. On the outfield billboard was an advertisement for French's mustard.

"What year is this, A1-33?" Jimmy asked.

"1964, Jimmy," the box seat responded.

"1964!" Jimmy exclaimed. "But it looks and feels like I've been here before."

"You have," explained A1-33. "You watched infield drills here with Bobby Richardson."

"Oh yeah." Jimmy said. "Why am I here now? There isn't a game going on."

"There will be later. Right now, you need to witness what every athlete experiences from time to time."

Jimmy thought for a second. He'd learned a lot of lessons since his father had brought home the box seat. Some he had learned from A1-33, and others from Sam and Mr. Whitehill. He also learned lessons that had nothing to do with baseball. Mom, Dad and Mrs. Rae had taught him what his Mom called "life lessons." What was this new thing he had to see, he wondered.

"Jimmy, walk out to the field toward the Yankee dugout," A1-33 instructed.

"I can't do that," said Jimmy. "They'll throw me out of the stadium!"

"No one can see you, it's okay."

Jimmy looked toward the field and back to A1-33. He still didn't quite believe nobody could see him. He could see all of them, after all.

"Are you sure?" Jimmy asked.

"Go ahead," A1-33 encouraged.

Jimmy slowly walked down the stadium steps. When he got to the bottom, he hopped over the fence and landed in the on-deck circle. Jimmy walked toward the first base dugout. As he approached the steps, he peered into it and then stopped. What he saw inside made a huge smile form across his face.

Jimmy could recognize this Yankee anywhere, at anytime, and at any place. Sitting on the bench, staring at his glove was Dad's all-time favorite Yankee. It was the switch-hitting outfielder, Mickey Mantle!

Jimmy watched and studied Number Seven closely. Mickey Mantle seemed uneasy, like something was bothering him. Suddenly, a door inside the dugout opened. Out came the great Yankee player and manager, Yogi Berra.

"Come on, Mick. Relax, will you?" said Yogi Berra.

"I can't. I feel like the pennant is hanging over me," said Mickey Mantle. "All of New York is waiting for me to hit a record setting home run."

"All of New York? How about all of America?" shouted Mr. Berra.

"You're a big help," Mr. Mantle said.

Yogi Berra started to chuckle. He walked over to Mickey and started to talk to him in an assuring voice. That's just how Mr. Whitehill talks to us, thought Jimmy.

"Look, you're one of the greatest ball players of all time," said Yogi. "You became that way because of hard work, a lot of practice, and great skill. You'll hit that home run, Mick, but not by worrying about it. It's natural to feel the way you do. Just relax and play ball and you'll be fine."

Jimmy saw Mickey smiling as Yogi walked away. Just before Yogi got to the door, he turned back.

"Hey, Mick! Do me a favor?" asked Yogi.

"Sure." Mickey replied. "What type of favor?"

"Well, a homerun for starters," said Yogi. "But I don't care what records you break. I just want to win today's game."

Mickey Mantle tossed his glove at his manager. Jimmy was stunned, but both Yankee legends began to laugh. Mickey and Yogi walked through the door together, and into the locker room corridor. As the door closed, Jimmy lost sight of Number Seven and Number Eight.

Jimmy quickly jumped back into the stands and ran up to A1-33.

"I just saw Mickey Mantle," shouted Jimmy. "I can't believe it!"

"How was he doing?" asked A1-33.

"Well, I think he was nervous, and feeling pressure about hitting a home run. Then Yogi Berra came out and told Mickey that he's supposed to be nervous."

"That's right, Jimmy," said the box seat. "What do you think about that?"

"If Mickey Mantle can get nervous, I don't mind feeling that way also," said Jimmy. "Yogi says it's only human. Those guys are so cool. Yogi even started kidding around, and Mickey threw his glove at him, just like the guys and I do."

"You see Jimmy, ball players and athletes are just people. Now I want you to prepare hard for the game, and always give it your best. That's all you could ever ask of yourself."

All of a sudden Jillie came running into the room.

"Wake up Jimmy! It's nine o'clock," shouted his sister.

As Jimmy opened his eyes, he saw his little sister wearing a long dress and carrying one of his dad's golf clubs. Jimmy sat up in bed.

"Why are you dressed up?" Jimmy asked.

"I'm pretending I'm Little Bo Peep," answered Jillie.

"Are you excited about going to Cooperstown?"

"Yes," said Jillie with enthusiasm. "Are you excited about going to Story Book Village?"

"Very excited!" said Jimmy.

Jimmy then leaned over and said, "Baaah," imitating a sheep. Jillie laughed.

CHAPTER 26

Looking out of his bedroom window, Jimmy could see the weather was perfect for a ball game. Even though Jimmy was a bit nervous, he was looking forward to playing, winning, and having fun. He took his time putting on his uniform. Somehow, he felt A1-33 was watching over him and was as excited as he was about the big game.

Dad knocked on his son's door, entered the room, and sat on the bed.

"Jimmy, your mom and I are real proud of the way you've played this year. You've made plays and hit the ball better than any kid I've seen."

"Thanks, Dad," said Jimmy glancing toward A1-33. "I've had some great coaching."

"Mr. Whitehill is a great coach, but you've dedicated yourself to practice. You tried as hard as you could. No matter what happens today, win or lose, make the All-Star team or not, your mom and I think you're a winner."

Jimmy's father stood up, tapped Jimmy on the head, and walked out of the bedroom.

"Hey, Dad," Jimmy called. "We're going to win today, and I'm going to make the All-Star team. Do you know why?"

"Why?" his father asked surprised.

"Because I want it. I want it more than anything," Jimmy said.

Jimmy and his dad both smiled. Dad walked downstairs, and Jimmy finished suiting up. As he prepared to leave his room, Jimmy walked over to A1-33. He picked up the stadium seat and turned it around so that it faced the window.

"I thought this would make it easier for you today," said Jimmy. "I hope that someday I can do something to help you as much as you've helped me."

Suddenly, Jimmy saw a flash from A1-33's brass plate reflect in the window. At that moment, Jimmy knew more than ever A1-33 needed something from him as well. Sam had said A1-33 has a dream. Jimmy didn't know what it was he could do to help his friend, but he did know that someday he would figure it out.

A few minutes later, the McNeil family all piled into their car and headed off to the ballpark. Jimmy's dad wanted to get there early. He was expecting a big crowd and wanted to be sure he would get a good parking space.

As Dad parked the car, Jimmy looked out of the window toward the field. Sitting in the stands on the third base line was Sam.

"Look, Dad! Sam's already here," shouted Jimmy.

"I'm not surprised. Sam was at the stadium this week, and all he could talk about was this game," said Dad. "I think Sam's forgotten about the New York Yankees. The Blue Sox are his new home team."

Jimmy jumped out of the car, hustled over to Mr. Whitehill, and joined some of the other team members. Jimmy's team went out on the field to take practice. Within a few minutes, the Community Bank players appeared. Mr. Whitehill and the manager of Community Bank had agreed to split the practice time.

Larry Barnes was warming up on the first base line. Jimmy was trying not to watch him, but he noticed Barnes seemed unusually quiet. He threw pitch after pitch, focusing his eyes intently on the catcher. Not one wise crack came out of his mouth.

Mr. Whitehill called the team into the dugout to read the line-up. This would be the third pitching match of the season between Bobby Sharples and Larry Barnes. There would be a few changes in the line-up since Ricky wasn't going to make the game. Brennan Jones was coming off the bench and was playing left field. Stanley Johnson moved to second, and Jimmy was going to play shortstop.

Jimmy started thinking about how Ricky must be feeling. The team was going to miss him today. Not only because of his playing ability, but also because of the way he kept everyone's spirits up all the time. We have to win this game for him, Jimmy thought.

Community Bank took the field, and the umpire walked over to the Blue Sox dugout.

"Let's get a batter up and one in the on-deck circle," said the umpire to Mr. Whitehill.

Mr. Whitehill nodded and tapped Joey on the back. The big game was starting!

Bobby Sharples took his place in the on-deck circle, and Jimmy grabbed his helmet and bat. For the first time, he would be up third. Everything felt so different. Jimmy was confident, though. He knew he was prepared for the game.

Mr. Whitehill directed the team to wait for Larry Barnes to throw a strike before they swung. His strategy was to make Barnes throw a lot of pitches, and tire him early. Mr. Whitehill understood what a great pitcher Larry could be when his head was in the game.

Barnes's first pitch was right down the middle, and Joey had the green light to hit the next pitch. Two pitches later, Joey hit a chopper to the shortstop, who made an easy play to first for the out. Sharples stepped up to home plate, and Jimmy moved into the on-deck circle. Bobby Sharples also took the first pitch, which was a perfectly thrown strike.

Barnes is on today, Jimmy thought. The next pitch thrown to Sharples was a little high, but Bobby swung anyway. The ball popped up to the first baseman and was caught for the second out.

Jimmy entered the batter's box, determined to get on base. Barnes had not thrown a bad pitch yet. Jimmy wondered if he should jump on the first one, but quickly decided against it. Mr. Whitehill had given specific instructions about taking the first strike.

Barnes stood tall on the mound. He looked directly into the catcher's glove. He went into his wind up and fired a fastball. As Jimmy watched it go by, he knew the umpire was going to call strike one.

"Strike one!" hollered the umpire.

"Okay, Jimmy. It's all yours now," called Mr. Whitehill. "Swing at a good pitch."

Jimmy dug his back foot into position, and waited for Barnes's next fireball. As the pitch came in, Jimmy followed it closely. The ball was moving a little bit to the inside and Jimmy decided not to swing.

"Strike two," yelled the umpire.

Jimmy had known it would be a close pitch, but he didn't feel comfortable swinging at it.

"You have him now, Larry. One more pitch and you retire them," encouraged Community Bank's manager.

Barnes started his wind up, Jimmy held his bat steady, and the next pitch thrown was in the strike zone. Jimmy's bat came off his shoulder and squarely met the ball. The ball screamed off the bat. It was a hard hit line drive down the third base line. Jimmy's initial instincts were that this was going to be in for extra bases.

But before Jimmy could even move both feet out of the batter's box, José Sanchez, Community Bank's third baseman extended his glove and snagged the ball on the fly.

Jimmy's entire team looked stunned as Community Bank cheered Jose's incredible catch. The Sox had gone down in order. Barnes was pitching great, and the defense looked sharp. Jimmy had a feeling that this was going to be one tough ballgame.

Joey Petruto came out of the dugout and tossed Jimmy his glove. Jimmy grabbed it, turned, and hustled out to shortstop. It felt odd to be positioned there. He had been trained as a second baseman.

Jimmy looked toward the bleachers and caught Sam looking at him. He was gently nodding his head toward Jimmy, as if he were telling him, it's okay, just concentrate.

The left-handed hitter José Sanchez came up to bat.

"Stanley, move over more to your left," Jimmy yelled, remembering how Sanchez hit.

Stanley listened, and David Rockman helped position him correctly as well.

The ball went to Sharples on the mound. He slowly stepped off the rubber, and then turned and looked toward his teammates in the field. Bobby was ready to pitch, and everyone could see the determination on his face.

"All yours, Bobby! No hitter," Jimmy cheered.

The rest of the team joined in. Bobby smiled, stepped up to the pitcher's rubber, and entered into his wind-up. He kicked toward home plate, and then threw the hardest fastball anyone had ever seen him hurl. The ball blazed by the batter for a called strike one. Jimmy could see Mike Laffey shaking his glove hand after receiving the pitch.

Bobby threw two more identical pitches, striking out José for the first out.

The next batter barely made contact with Sharples' second pitch. He hit a little grounder in front of home plate. Mike Laffey jumped on it and threw to first for out number two.

Larry Barnes was now up to bat. If anyone could do damage to the Blue Sox with a bat, it was Larry. Sharples walked around the mound a couple of times, and then enthusiastically jumped back on the rubber. Mr. Whitehill called for the outfield to take a few steps backwards. He then waved to Jimmy to move toward the back of the infield dirt.

The count on Barnes quickly went to 1-2. Jimmy crouched into position and watched as Bobby threw. Barnes began his swing. Right away, Jimmy could see that contact was going to be made. The bat was whipping around fast. Jimmy started to take steps sideways to his right, anticipating that the ball would be hit there.

Barnes slammed a ground ball toward Joey at third. The ball was hit so hard, Joey hardly had time to move. His glove hand made an attempt to field the ball, but it bounced off the outside of his mitt. Jimmy was steadily moving toward his right. The ball ricocheted off of Joey, and was running directly to Jimmy. He knew he had to hurry.

Jimmy quickly scooped the ball up. He pivoted and threw toward

David Rockman at first.

The turning motion of his body caused him to throw side arm. The ball looked like it would beat Barnes to first, but it was dropping low. Rockman stretched his body out as far as he could and extended his glove. As the ball hit the ground in front of him, David's eyes never left the ball. His glove closed on it, and then came upward, showing the umpire he had it.

"Out!" The ump yelled.

Mr. Whitehill jumped out of the dugout to celebrate the close call. As the Blue Sox headed into the dugout, Jimmy looked up into the stands and saw everyone cheering. Sam tipped his hat and gave him a big smile.

The next few innings proved to be the usual pitcher's duel between Larry Barnes and Bobby Sharples. Through three complete innings, both pitchers had perfect games. Not one batter on either team had reached first base!

In the top of the fourth, the Sox were back to the beginning of their line-up. Jimmy knew that if one of them could get on base, Rockman would be sure to knock him in.

Larry Barnes was throwing all strikes, and Mr. Whitehill had now instructed the team to swing at any pitch they were comfortable with, even if it was the first one thrown. Joey swung at the first two pitches and missed completely. Jimmy could see that he was getting frustrated. Joey fouled the third pitch and then took the fourth one for a called strike.

Bobby Sharples walked to the plate. He patted Joey on the back as he steamed into the dugout.

"Come on, Bobby! Win your own game," Mr. Whitehill yelled.

"Let's go, Bobby!" yelled Jimmy. "Get a base hit."

On the first pitch thrown, Bobby hit a sharp ground ball to the short-stop. He made a clean play, and quickly went to throw the ball. As he pulled the ball out of his glove, his hand couldn't hold on to it firmly, and the ball fell to the ground. Bobby ran as hard as he could and was safe at first.

The shortstop's play was ruled an error, and Barnes' perfect game was over.

Everyone in the dugout rose to their feet as Jimmy came up to the plate. Jimmy looked toward Mr. Whitehill. To his surprise, Jimmy's manager was giving him the bunt sign. Why would he want me to bunt, wondered Jimmy? If I sacrifice myself, there'll be two outs. I know I can hit the ball and move Bobby around.

Jimmy settled himself in the batter's box. Community Bank's third baseman was playing way back. Jimmy knew he should send the bunt down that way, because it would be the toughest play. As Barnes wound up, Jimmy quickly flashed back to his Yankee bunting drill. Jimmy squared around, and the third and first baseman started to charge forward.

Barnes' pitch was moving fast. Jimmy pushed his bat forward to meet the ball, and directed it to the right of the third baseman. He made contact, and the ball headed exactly in that direction. He took off in a flash, never looking at the ball.

"Hurry!" Mr. Roshay yelled from the first base coach's box.

Jimmy knew it would be close. His legs were moving as fast as he could. He saw the second baseman covering first, and he was starting to extend his body outward as if he were going to catch the ball. Jimmy's foot hit the bag and then he heard the thump of the ball in the second baseman's glove.

"Safe," yelled the umpire.

Jimmy's momentum brought him to the edge of the outfield. As he headed back to first, Mr. Roshay congratulated him.

"What happened?" Jimmy asked.

"Great bunt, Jimmy. That was a base hit," said Mr. Roshay. "You broke up the no-hitter, and put Bobby into scoring position."

Community Bank's manager, Mr. Harrison, called time out and walked toward the mound. He waved in the catcher to join the conversation.

"What are they doing?" Jimmy asked Mr. Roshay.

"I don't know, but I have a feeling they don't want to pitch to David Rockman," said the coach.

Larry Barnes was nodding his head as he listened intently to his manager. Finally, the manager jogged back to the dugout, and the umpire hollered, "Let's go!"

Barnes went to the pitching rubber, and Rockman stood in the batter's box. Community Bank's catcher extended his right arm out, indicating an intentional walk. Barnes then threw the ball outside and wide of home plate. The catcher calmly stepped to his right and caught the ball.

"Ball one," called the umpire to nobody's surprise.

David Rockman put the bat by his side and began to stare at Larry Barnes. David then started talking under his breath. He definitely wanted to hit the ball.

"Stand ready in the batter's box, David!" Mr. Whitehill yelled. "He may decide to throw you a strike."

David listened to Mr. Whitehill's advice, but a strike was never thrown. Four straight intentional balls came, and David headed to first base. Jimmy advanced to second and Bobby to third. The bases were loaded with only one out.

Mike Laffey walked up to the plate, and Larry Barnes proceeded to throw three blazing pitches. Mike swung and missed all three. Stanley Johnson then took his turn. Standing at second base, Jimmy felt like he was watching an instant replay on TV. Barnes reached back and again threw three straight past Johnson. The inning was over, and the Blue Sox had left three runners stranded on base.

Community Bank surrounded Barnes, congratulating him for his great pitching, while the Sox quietly took their positions out in the field.

It was the bottom of the fourth, and Community Bank had the top of their line-up coming to the plate. Sanchez was up, and Stanley Johnson remembered he was a pull hitter. He moved over without having to be reminded.

Sanchez popped up for the first out, and Bobby struck out the next batter. Bobby had retired eleven straight batters, and still had a perfect game.

Larry Barnes entered the batter's box. Instinctively, every player in the field took a couple of steps back. Jimmy went into his crouched infield position and concentrated on the pitch. Bobby missed the strike zone on both of his first two pitches, and seemed to be getting jittery. He didn't want to give Barnes anything too good to swing at. Bobby had to make sure that this one was in the strike zone.

Bobby delivered a fastball down the middle and Barnes took a mighty cut. The ball slammed off the bat way up into the air. Everyone turned around and followed the ball as it easily cleared the left center field fence. The homerun hit the top of the trees twenty feet behind the fences.

Jimmy's head dropped to the ground. He then looked up at Bobby, who stood on the pitcher's mound in a daze. Barnes was making his way around the bases with a big grin on his face. The sound of Community Bank's fans cheering was like thunder. Larry Barnes, in just one swing, had broken up Bobby's perfect game, no hitter, and shut out.

Worst of all, Community Bank had taken the game's lead with only two innings left to play. Jimmy began to worry. What if they beat us like they did last time, he wondered? I can't lose my confidence, he thought.

I need to keep my head in the game.

Community Bank's next batter hit a chopper to Rockman at first. David made an easy play and the side was retired. The defense jogged into the dugout knowing they needed to score some runs and soon.

In the fifth inning, the pitchers seemed to be in complete control of the game, as both sides were retired one, two, and three. This brought the game into what could be the last and final inning of the season.

Mr. Whitehill gathered everyone in the dugout, they each took their place on the bench.

"You've all played hard this season," said Mr. Whitehill. "Sometimes in an athlete's career, there comes a time when he or she needs to reach down deep inside and pull out a play they didn't even know they were capable of making."

The team nodded.

"This is one of those times," the manager continued. "This could be your last opportunity to prove to all of your classmates, friends, and family that you are the best team in this league. This inning, we have the top of our line-up at bat. Now let's get a whole bunch of runs and put this game out of reach!"

David Rockman let out a big cheer, and the rest of the team joined in with encouragement.

Joey walked toward home plate, and fans from both teams started cheering. Joey had struck out on a called third strike his last time up, and he wasn't about to let it happen again.

Mr. Whitehill encouraged Joey from the third base coach's box. Joey set himself in the batter's box, while Barnes stepped onto the pitching rubber. Joey was anxious to get a hit and fouled off the first two pitches. The third pitch was on the outside, but Joey swung anyhow, somehow connecting with the ball. He hit a high pop up to the second baseman.

"Run, Joey! Run!" Mr. Whitehill yelled.

The ball was still up in the air, while Joey was tearing his way down the first base path. All eyes were on Community Bank's second baseman as he tried to position himself under the ball. He stepped to his left, and then stepped to his right, then back to his left. Joey had almost reached first base when the second baseman made his way under the ball.

The second baseman's glove was facing upward. As his hands went up, the ball slammed into his mitt, but bounced upward in the air. A hush fell over the crowd. The second baseman again placed his glove hand out. This time the ball landed softly in his mitt like a feather floating into a basket.

Everyone in the Blue Sox dugout dropped his head as the umpire announced the out.

Bobby Sharples started his trip up to the plate, as Jimmy moved toward the on-deck circle. Mr. Whitehill called time out, trotted toward Bobby, and spoke with him. Jimmy couldn't hear what was being said. Bobby nodded his head and then entered the batter's box. Jimmy looked at Mr. Whitehill and knew he had something up his sleeve.

Barnes delivered the pitch and Bobby laid a bunt down the first base line. The catcher charged the ball, scooped it up, and hurled it to first base well in time to get the out. Bobby ran through first base and then walked into the dugout. He turned around and looked at Jimmy.

"It's up to you, Jimmy," he hollered. "You can do it, Jimmy. You can do it!"

This is it. There are two outs, Jimmy thought. If I don't get on base, the season's over and we're in second place. He felt nervous, like he was carrying the world upon his shoulders. He stood frozen in the on-deck circle.

"Batter up," yelled the umpire.

"Jimmy, it's okay. You know exactly what to do."

Jimmy turned around. It was Sam's voice, and he was standing at the fence.

"Jimmy, remember all you've learned this season," said Sam. "Everything from batting to having fun. It's natural to feel anxious right now. Think of all the great ball players you've watched. You can do it!"

Sam turned away and walked back to his seat.

"Let's go, batter!" The umpire yelled.

Jimmy started his stroll toward home plate. He faintly heard the cheering of his team, coaches, and fans. His mind was flashing back to every lesson he had learned from A1-33. The thought of how special his training was seemed to fire energy inside of him. He stepped into the batter's box and stared directly into the eyes of Larry Barnes.

Barnes quickly went into a wind up and delivered his first pitch. The ball looked like it was moving low and away. Jimmy's eyes followed it closely. He decided not to swing.

"Ball one," called the umpire.

Jimmy heard a roar from his dugout.

Larry Barnes quickly fired his next pitch. The ball was moving hard and seemed to be outside. Again, Jimmy chose not to swing.

"Strike one," called the ump.

A cheer came from the Community Bank dugout this time.

Jimmy stepped out of the batter's box, and decided to take a breath.

He looked at David Rockman in the on-deck circle.

"Just get on. Jimmy," said David. "I'll bring you in from there!"

Jimmy knew David meant every word. He had to get on base. Jimmy jumped back into the batter's box. He shifted his back foot and locked himself in place, ready for Barnes' pitch.

The league's top pitcher went into his wind up. As his arms came over the top of his shoulders, Jimmy watched his hand release the ball. The pitch was straight down the middle. Jimmy stepped forward. His left leg opened his hips as he went into his swing. Like a bullet, the ball exploded into a line drive that zipped over the third baseman's head. Jimmy put his head down and set his sights on first base. In front of him, Mr. Roshay was yelling, "Take two! Take two, Jimmy!"

As Jimmy rounded first and headed toward second, he could see that the left fielder was just barely getting to the ball. Jimmy easily reached second base for a double. As the ball came back to the infield, the umpire called for a time out.

The Blue Sox fans were on their feet cheering. Jimmy's teammates were now standing by the dugout fence, anxiously waiting to see what would happen next. As Jimmy stood on second base, he saw Rockman making his way to the batter's box. Jimmy's eyes searched the stands for Sam.

In the middle of the cheering crowd, he found him. Standing with a smile, Sam tipped his Yankee hat to Jimmy in the traditional manner. This time, a flash of light seemed to bounce off Sam's hat.

Community Bank's manager was now on the mound talking to Barnes. There were two outs, and the tying run on second. The best hitter in the league stepped up to bat. Jimmy realized exactly what they were going to do. They were going to intentionally walk David. They wanted to pitch to Mike Laffey, who had struck out on three straight pitches his last time up.

"Batter up," yelled the umpire.

David Rockman had a fierce look on his face, and was ready to hit. Barnes was standing on the rubber. The catcher stood up and extended his right hand, calling for the intentional walk.

Larry Barnes threw the first pitch way left as the catcher had indicated.

"Ball one," the umpire said unenthusiastically under his breath.

The entire ballpark was in dead silence. The Blue Sox's hopes for winning the pennant were quickly dwindling away.

Standing impatiently in the batter's box, David broke the silence.

"Chicken," he called out loudly to Barnes.

Larry started to get fidgety on the mound. He then stepped up to the rubber and threw a second intentional ball.

Rockman put the end of his bat into the dirt and leaned on the handle. He moved the helmet off of his eyes so Barnes could clearly see them. He then yelled out, "Yellow!"

"Hey, my manager is making me do this," said Barnes. "I'm not afraid of you."

"Just pitch, Larry!" Mr. Harrison yelled from the dugout.

Barnes, who was still upset, delivered his third throw for ball three. The catcher threw the ball back to Larry, who stepped on the mound.

"Coward," David coaxed.

Barnes was angry, and he stepped right on the mound. Rockman knew exactly what he was doing and set himself in the batter's box, preparing for the pitch. Community Bank's catcher gave the signal for the intentional walk, but Barnes wound up and fired a pitch straight down the middle of the strike zone. Rockman's bat came whipping around. Like the sound of an explosion, the ball blasted its way into deep right center.

Jimmy took off like a rabbit toward third base. He was watching Mr. Whitehill, who was jumping up and down and cheering.

"It's gone! That ball is gone!" he yelled.

Jimmy quickly turned his head toward the outfield, and watched as the ball traveled over the fence. David Rockman was running, jumping, and waving his right arm high in the air. The crowd was going crazy with excitement. Jimmy hit home plate and waited for David to finish his home run trot.

The big guy stomped on home plate and jumped on Jimmy. Jimmy thought he was going to break in half. They had just taken the lead in what seemed like a miracle.

"Come on, guys. The game's not over," said Mr. Whitehill. "We're not ready to celebrate just yet."

Their manager was right, and Jimmy and his team knew it. As happy as they were, the game wasn't over. Mike Laffey grounded out to the third baseman for the third out. The Blue Sox took the field with a one run lead in the bottom of the sixth. Community Bank's eight, nine, and number one batters were coming up.

Bobby Sharples continued his pitching show. He struck out the first two batters. This put the team within one out of the league's championship. Community Bank's top of the line-up was now coming to home plate. The count went to 2-2 on Sanchez. Bobby reached back, looking for the game winning pitch.

José hit a ground ball between Rockman and Johnson at second base. Rockman came up with the ball and turned to throw, but no one was covering the bag. David took off toward first but was beaten by a step. José was safe with an infield hit.

There was a runner on first, with two outs, and the number two batter was up. Barnes stepped into the on-deck circle.

"Come on, Bobby. We need this out," Jimmy encouraged.

Bobby looked at Jimmy and nodded. He then stepped on the mound. The ballpark fell to a hush. It was so quiet, all you could hear was the sound of Bobby winding up as he delivered his first pitch.

"Ball one," yelled the umpire.

Community Bank's fans all cheered.

"Come on, Bobby. You can do it," Joey cheered.

Jimmy knew they had to get this out. They couldn't let Barnes get up to the plate for another chance, particularly with a runner in scoring position. The next delivery by Sharples was in the strike zone for a called strike one.

The Sox fans answered with a roaring cheer, and the count went to 1-1. Anticipate the play, Jimmy thought. Think about what you're going to do if you get the ball.

Jimmy crouched into position and Bobby threw the next pitch. The batter hit a sharp ground ball just to the left side of the pitcher's mound. Bobby made a stab at it with his glove but missed. Jimmy was moving to his left as the ball continued up the middle. Jimmy extended his glove hand out. It seemed as if he was not going to reach the ball. Jimmy quickly pushed off his feet and dove toward the ball. His glove came down right on top of it, but he had to finish the play.

His body had landed about two feet away from the second base bag. He looked up and saw José approaching quickly. Jimmy only had one chance. He reached outward with his mitt. Jimmy tagged the base and felt a heavy pressure on the outside of his glove. José had stepped on Jimmy's mitt!

Jimmy's hand hurt, but he wasn't worried about the pain. He had beat José to the bag, meaning only one thing; José was out!

José went sprawling on the ground over Jimmy, and landed in the infield dirt. Jimmy turned his head to see if José was okay.

"Out!" yelled the umpire.

"Nice play," José said.

"Thanks," said Jimmy.

Jimmy looked up, and his teammates were running toward him. The Blue Sox had won the game and the pennant!

Jimmy looked at his glove and smiled. He and his glove had made the big play to clinch the game. Suddenly he felt himself being lifted in the air. David Rockman had picked him up from behind, and the entire team had piled onto the field in celebration.

The crowd was on their feet cheering, and the Blue Sox players were jumping up and down and congratulating each other. After a while, Mr. Whitehill finally settled everyone down, including himself. The team gathered in the dugout for the final speech of the season.

"Next week, we will have a team party at Burgerville," announced their Manager. "As for right now, go home and have a great meal. You deserve it!"

"You do, too," said Bobby Sharples.

"Thanks, Bobby. But I have no time right now," said Mr. Whitehill. "All the coaches are getting ready to meet and select this year's All-Star team."

"It was a great season, guys," said Mr. Roshay. "Now I want all of you to line up and shake hands with Community Bank. They had a great season too."

The team did as their coach had instructed, and shook hands with all the players except one. Larry Barnes walked out of Welty Park by himself. Jimmy felt bad that Larry was all alone, but he didn't think it was right that he was acting like such a sore sport either.

Jimmy began his exit from the field, and saw his family waiting by the fence. Mom grabbed her son and gave him a hug. Jimmy quickly squirmed away out of embarrassment.

"We're really proud of all of you," Dad exclaimed.

Jimmy smiled at his father, and then looked up as Sam emerged through the crowd. Sam extended his hand out and put it on Jimmy's shoulder.

"Jimmy, you're the best I've ever seen," said Sam. "You have so much talent and potential. Don't ever give up your dream, and you'll someday be in Yankee pinstripes."

Jimmy looked up and smiled. It was one of the nicest things anyone had ever said to him.

Later that day when Jimmy got home, he called Ricky to let him know that they had won. Ricky was happy, but Jimmy could tell there was disappointment in his voice. Jimmy could understand how Ricky felt; after all, Ricky had been a big part of the team this year.

Jimmy entered his room and went over to A1-33, who was facing the window.

"Thank you, coach," Jimmy said. "If it weren't for you, I wouldn't be playing like I am. Thank you for everything you've taught me, and thank you in advance for all that I still have to learn."

Jimmy's one-way conversation was interrupted by a knock on the bedroom door. Jimmy turned around as his father entered the room. Dad had a solemn look on his face.

"What's up, Dad?" Jimmy asked.

"Well, I have good news and bad news for you," Dad said.

"What's the matter?"

"Well, let me give you the bad news first," said Dad. "It looks like we're going to have to delay our trip to Cooperstown till later this summer."

"Why?" Jimmy asked disappointedly.

"Because I just received a phone call from Mr. Whitehill, you made this year's traveling Little League All-Star team!"

CHAPTER 27

The way a team plays as a whole determines its success.
You may have the greatest bunch of individuals in the world,
but if they don't play together, the club won't be worth a dime.

–Babe Ruth

After completing two weeks of All-Star practice, the Yonkers team was looking strong. They had *great* talent. Mr. Whitehill was awarded the manager's position. Mr. Harrison, Community Bank's manager was his coach.

As usual, Mr. Whitehill held a lot of practices. He told the team they were good enough to make it all the way to Williamsport. After only a few practices, every player on the team believed it.

Jimmy decided to leave for Little League practice a little early and ride his bicycle over to Ricky's house. Ever since the pennant-winning game, Ricky had avoided him. He hadn't even shown up for the Blue Sox's season ending party. Ricky was one of his best friends, and Jimmy really wanted it to stay that way.

When he arrived at Ricky's house, Mrs. Birk answered the door, and told Jimmy that Ricky wasn't home. Jimmy was getting used to that response. He jumped back on his bike, and headed over to Welty Park for practice.

"Hey, Jimmy!" yelled David from behind him.

"What's going on?" Jimmy asked, while riding his bike.

"Oh, not too much," David said. "I'm ready for the first All-Star game."

"Yeah, me too," Jimmy said. "The team's really good."

"You know, with Larry Barnes and Bobby Sharples, we have a great pitching rotation."

Jimmy thought about what great pitchers Larry and Bobby were. Jimmy was worried Larry Barnes wouldn't be able to keep his cool, though.

David and Jimmy peddled their bikes as fast as they could, and got to Welty Park in no time flat.

Jimmy and David threw a ball for about twenty minutes before the rest of the team showed up. Mr. Whitehill and Mr. Harrison called everyone into the dugout for a team meeting. As they sat on the bench,

Jimmy looked around and noticed all the talent that was there.

From the Blue Sox there were Bobby Sharples, David Rockman, Michael Laffey, and himself. From Community Bank there were Larry Barnes, José Sanchez, and Kirby Bukowski. From the Main Street Grill were the Gutin Brothers, the remaining players were from other teams.

"Okay, guys," began Mr. Whitehill. "Saturday, July 18th, against Pelham will be our first game. Over the years they've had good ballplayers, and have done very well. The All-Star Tournament is in single elimination format. So if we lose one, we're out."

Jimmy thought about this. The team needed to play its best every game. If they all wanted to make it to Williamsport, they would need to gel and win as a team.

"Each game should be played like it's the championship," added Mr. Harrison. "Mr. Whitehill and I feel this is the best ball club this town has ever produced! Practice and playing together is the only way we can win and advance in the tournament."

The team cheered, and hustled onto the playing field. The team started by working on cutoff throws from the outfield. The team continued to work hard all day fielding balls, taking batting-practice, and going through drills.

When practice was over, David and Jimmy walked over to their bikes. Much to their surprise, Sam and Jimmy's father were leaning on the fence.

"Hey, Pop! Hi, Sam!" Jimmy said happily. "What are you guys doing here?" "Actually, we have a surprise for you and David," Sam answered.

"A surprise?" Jimmy asked.

"Just wait until you hear this," Dad said. "Remember Mr. Graf from the Yankee office?"

"Sure. He was the man who I spoke to about the Yankee Monuments the day that I visited the stadium with you," said Jimmy.

Jimmy's father smiled and looked at Sam.

"That's right," Dad said. "Well, he came down to the stadium today. The Yankees are playing the Oakland Athletics tonight at Shea Stadium, and he gave me four tickets for the game. We thought it would be fun for you and David to join us. You guys interested?"

"Are you kidding?" asked David. "I'd love too! Except, I have to check with my parents first."

"Jimmy's mom spoke with your mother about an hour ago," Dad said. "She said have a great time."

"Wow!" blurted out David.

Jimmy's father instructed David and Jimmy to drop off their bikes and get ready to go. Jimmy's father had picked up some of David's clothes from his mother so he could spend the night. Jimmy and David excitedly drove to Jimmy's house to get ready. The whole ride back they talked about who their favorite Yankee players were.

Jimmy and David had a great time at the game. Sam noted that in all his years as an usher, he had never seen anyone eat more than David! It was almost midnight when they finally arrived at the McNeil house. David and Jimmy went straight to Jimmy's room. They were so tired they headed right to bed. Jimmy's mother had set up a mattress and sheets for David to sleep on. As David was climbing into bed, he stared at A1-33.

"Wow! Is that the stadium seat you've been talking about?" David asked. "You're really lucky to have it."

"Thanks," said Jimmy. "So you like it?"

"Yeah, it's great!"

Jimmy didn't tell David any more about the box seat. He didn't want to tell anyone beside Sam about all of the wonderful and crazy things that happened with him and A1-33. Jimmy wondered if anyone else could really understand.

The two buddies fell asleep quickly that evening. Before they knew it, Jimmy's mom was waking them up for breakfast. On the way downstairs to the kitchen, David turned to Jimmy.

"You won't believe the dream I had last night," David said.

"Dream? What about a dream?" Jimmy asked astonished.

"It was so cool," said David. "I was playing football for the Giants, and I was at the new stadium they're building in New Jersey, and it was a playoff game! I was a linebacker and, well, I intercepted a pass at the thirty-five yard line and ran it all the way back for a touchdown!"

"Wow," Jimmy said. "What a dream, a kid winning a playoff game!"

"No, that's the thing. I wasn't a kid," explained David. "I was a grown up. It was so real I thought I was there."

Jimmy looked at David and smiled. The two took their places around the breakfast table as Mom dished out the food.

"Dreams can be great," David said. "Don't you think?"

"Definitely," responded Jimmy.

CHAPTER 28

On August 18, 1975, the local newspaper, the *Herald-Statesman,* ran the following article about the Yonkers Little League All-Star team on the front page:

Barnes and Sharples Lead Little Leaguers to Williamsport.

YONKERS. A team of baseball players made city history yesterday by advancing to the Little League All-Star Tournament. The team has been led by the outstanding one-two pitching punch of the right-handed Larry Barnes and lefty Bobby Sharples.

The team has had its share of hitting success as well. First baseman, David Rockman, is leading the team with a tournament batting average of .400, 3 home runs and 12 RBIs. The shortstop, Jimmy McNeil, is batting .356 with four stolen bases. McNeil has been very impressive defensively thus far in the tournament.

The team will travel by bus this Friday, August 20th, to Williamsport, Pennsylvania where they will face teams from all over the United States and around the world. As always, pro scouts will attend the tournament from most major league organizations.

All of us from the *Herald-Statesman* would like to wish our Little Leaguers the best of luck. We all hope they make it to the final game, and bring home the World Championship.

CHAPTER 29

"Jimmy, have you finished packing yet?" Mom asked.

"No, I'll do it now," Jimmy returned.

The entire house was buzzing with excitement. Dad had gone to the train station to pick up Sam. Sam had said he wouldn't miss the Williamsport Tournament for anything, and Sam never went back on his word. Jimmy was riding in a bus with the team to Williamsport, while Mom, Dad, Jillie, and Sam were going to follow in the car.

As Jimmy packed his gear, he looked at A1-33.

"I wish you were coming to Williamsport with me," Jimmy said to A1-33. "Leaving you behind is kind of like leaving my good luck charm."

Jimmy paused. Professional athletes had good luck charms. Why couldn't he? Jimmy rushed downstairs to talk to his mother.

"What's the matter, Jimmy?" asked Mom, once he got downstairs.

"Nothing at all, if you let me bring A1-33 to Williamsport," said Jimmy.

"Bring your stadium seat? Now why would you want to do that?"

"Because it's a good luck charm," Jimmy said.

"I really don't think that's such a good idea," Mom said. "There's hardly any room in the car already. Where would we put it?"

"I'll take it on the bus with me."

Jimmy's Mom looked at her son and sighed.

"If it is that important to you, then I suppose it can't hurt," Mom said. "But be careful. Your seat is a very important piece of memorabilia, and it is also means a lot to Sam."

"I'll be very careful," Jimmy returned. "A1-33 is very important to me too."

By the time Dad came home with Sam, Jimmy, his suitcase, his gym bag, and A1-33 were downstairs and waiting to go.

Sam walked into the house and looked at the stadium seat sitting next to Jimmy's suitcase. "Are you bringing A1-33 along?" Sam asked cautiously.

"Yes," Jimmy said hesitantly. "Do you think that's wrong?"

"No, I understand why you want to bring A1-33. Just be very careful," Sam returned.

"Listen to the two of you," said Dad. "You make it sound like the stadium seat is a person!" Jimmy looked at Sam, but neither one of them responded to the comment.

The McNeil family drove to the parking lot at Welty Park, and Jimmy boarded the team bus with the rest of the players. As he climbed onto the bus, Jimmy was carrying his gym bag and A1-33. It was a bit clumsy trying to carry his stadium seat and bag down the bus' small aisle.

"Hey, what are you carrying?" Kirby Bukowski, the team's second baseman, asked.

"Oh, just a good luck charm of mine," Jimmy returned.

All of a sudden, Jimmy began to think it was a mistake bringing A1-33 along. As fast as the thought flashed through his mind, Jimmy heard the annoying voice of Larry Barnes.

"Good luck charm, huh?" asked Larry. "Is that your secret, McNeil?"

"What do you mean, secret?" Jimmy snapped back.

"Well, I knew it had to be something that helped your game," returned Larry. "You didn't have the talent to make the All-Star team on your own!"

A few of the players began to crack up. Jimmy felt heat building up inside him, like he was getting ready to explode. He was about to say something to Barnes when his left hand, which was gripping A1-33, felt a strange sensation. Instantly, Jimmy's mind thought back to Lou Gehrig and how he had dealt with fans at Yankee Stadium. Jimmy quickly composed himself. The bus was silent, waiting for his response to Barnes.

"Yeah Barnes, if it wasn't for this seat, right now I'd be waving to you guys from the street," said Jimmy.

His answer made everyone laugh, and eased his embarrassment. David Rockman waved to Jimmy as he continued his walk down the aisle.

"I saved a seat for you," said David. "But where are you going to put A1-33?"

Mr. Whitehill, who had been listening to the entire conversation, came over and tried to take A1-33 from Jimmy. Jimmy tightened his grip.

"Hey, it's okay," said Mr. Whitehill. "I'm just going to put your seat in an empty row."

"Oh, sorry," said Jimmy. "I'm just a little protective. This means a lot to me."

"I understand, Jimmy."

Jimmy handed the box seat over to his manager. Mr. Whitehill then turned to the team and said, "You know, guys, some pros don't wash their socks or shave when they're on hitting streaks. Some of the best athletes have good luck charms. We're playing great ball, but a little good luck never hurt."

The sound of the engine roared as the driver started the bus. Mr. Whitehill instructed everyone to settle into his seat. The manager then went outside and spoke to the parents and fans that were following the bus in their own cars. Through the back window, David and Jimmy counted twenty-one cars in all.

The trip to Williamsport, Pennsylvania took about five hours. Most of the players thought it went pretty quick, though Mr. Whitehill and Mr. Harrison thought it took forever. The bus pulled up in front of the Sheraton Hotel where the team was staying. Hanging from the awning of the hotel was a big banner that read, "Welcome Little League All-Star Regional Winners."

As soon as the players saw the sign, they busted out cheering.

David Rockman started yelling, "We're number one. We're number one."

Soon the rest of the team was cheering too. It took Mr. Whitehill a while to quiet everyone down and get the team off the bus.

As the team entered the lobby, they noticed the entire hotel staff was dressed in baseball uniforms. It appeared they were as excited about the All-Stars staying in their hotel as the teams were. Dad found Jimmy in the crowd, and instructed him to wait with his Mom, Jillie, and Sam. As soon as Jillie saw Jimmy, she came running over to him with a big smile on her face.

"Let's go swimming," Jillie said.

Mom and Sam both began to laugh.

"Jimmy's going down to the ball field with the team, Jillie," Mom said. "But you and I can go down to the pool after we get checked in."

Sam quickly grabbed Jimmy to the side. He bent down to talk with him quietly.

"Where's A1-33?" Sam asked.

"On the bus," Jimmy returned.

"You can't leave the seat there," Sam said, with a concerned sound to his voice.

"I won't. I'll get him when Dad has our room keys."

"No, Jimmy. I think you should get him now."

Jimmy could tell how serious Sam sounded, and he quickly agreed. Jimmy walked out of the hotel lobby, and saw the bus driver pulling luggage out of the bus' side compartments. The door to the bus was open, and Jimmy walked up the steps. As he turned left into the aisle, he saw that Larry Barnes had picked up A1-33.

"What are you doing with my stadium seat?" Jimmy asked.

"Ah, nothing," Larry said with a suprised sound in his voice.

"Nothing?" Jimmy asked sternly. "Then why is it in your hands?"

"I wanted to see what it looks like, McNeil. Just relax. I wouldn't do anything to hurt your good luck charm. After all, we're on the same team."

"That's right, Larry. We are on the same team."

Jimmy took A1-33 from Larry, and exited the bus. Waiting on the sidewalk was Sam. His eyes went right to A1-33. He then looked over Jimmy's shoulder and saw Barnes.

"Everything okay?" Sam asked slowly.

"Yeah, everything's okay," said Jimmy. "You were right, though. I found Larry Barnes holding A1-33."

"Well as long as you have it now," said Sam. "Your Mom and Dad are looking for you. They're waiting inside. We all have our room keys. Let me take A1-33 from you while you help your Dad with the luggage."

Jimmy handed A1-33 over to Sam. Larry Barnes walked by the two of them and entered into the hotel lobby.

"Make sure you keep A1-33 away from Larry in the future," said Sam. "I have a bad feeling about him."

"I think it was a mistake bringing A1-33 with us," Jimmy said. "It seems to be creating a problem."

"No, A1-33 belongs here. It's not a problem. You just need to be very, very careful."

Everyone checked into his or her room, and then the team gathered back in front of the hotel. Mr. Whitehill was bringing the All-Stars down to the Little League stadium so they could see the field they would be playing on. Ordinarily, Mr. Whitehill would take advantage of this time and hold a practice, but there were special times allocated for each team.

The team piled back onto the bus to prepare for their tour of Lamade Stadium. Mr. Whitehill made an announcement that the trip to the field would be a short one, since tonight they were to attend a banquet at the hotel. Teams from all around the world would be at the gathering.

The hotel was only a few minutes from the fields. Out of the window of the bus, Jimmy could see down a long grass-covered hill leading to seven fields, including one that looked like a tiny major league stadium. As the bus pulled into the parking lot and got closer to the Little League Stadium, the chatter on the bus fell to silence. Mr. Whitehill, who was sitting in the front seat, stood up and faced the team as soon as the bus came to a stop.

"I want all of you to very slowly and quietly leave the bus in single file and follow me," said their manager.

Each and every one of the ballplayers did as Mr. Whitehill had directed. Danny Gutin was the first player to follow their manager. The team was absolutely quiet as they piled out of the bus in single file. Barnes was three players behind Mr. Whitehill, and under his breath, Jimmy heard him say, "This is really weird."

"I think this is cool," returned David Rockman.

"Me too," whispered Jimmy.

"Quiet back there," said Mr. Harrison, and a hush fell over the team.

They continued following Mr. Whitehill through the entrance of the stadium. The group came to a halt at the backstop behind home plate. Mr. Whitehill began to speak, and everyone listened.

"If we play hard enough and are fortunate enough during the next seven days," said Mr. Whitehill, "we'll be playing in the final game of the Little League World Series."

Jimmy eagerly looked over at David who was smiling.

"There are only eight teams in the whole world that have advanced this far in the tournament," continued the manager. "It's an accomplishment of yours that you should always remember. The teams you'll play against will be much better than what you've faced so far. Remember, you'll be better than what they've faced as well."

"There are four teams from the US and four teams from foreign countries," added Mr. Harrison. "This is truly a World Series. I want each and every one of you to know how proud Mr. Whitehill and I are of you."

"But there is one thing I want you all to do right now," said Mr. Whitehill. "Look straight-away to center field."

Everyone turned their head as Mr. Whitehill pointed to the electronic scoreboard.

"One week from tomorrow, I want to see US East Team 5, Opponent 0," said Mr. Whitehill. "Can you do it?"

"Yes," the team answered back.

"You're not convincing me. Can you do it?"

"Yes," the team called, even louder.

"One more time," Mr. Whitehill said, "are you world champions?"

"Yes!" shouted the team so loud it probably rang through Williamsport.

"Good! Now let's get back on the bus feeling like champions!"

During the ride back to the hotel, the team was as pumped up as anyone had ever seen them. Mr. Whitehill reminded everyone of the banquet at six o'clock. When it was over, he wanted everyone back in his room immediately. He also reminded the team of practice at 8 a.m. the next morning.

Jimmy rushed back to his room to tell everyone about their trip to Lamade Stadium. As he started to speak, Mom urged him to get ready for the tournament banquet.

The McNeil family, including Sam, entered the ballroom at exactly 6 p.m. On the middle of each table were six balloons that looked like baseballs. Quickly they scurried through the crowd looking for the tables with their team's name on it.

Mom found the right table, and they all took their seats. David Rockman and his parents, along with Mr. Whitehill, joined them. The banquet began with speeches that Jimmy thought were pretty boring. The food was good, though. There was a giant table with everything from fried chicken to lasagna on it.

The banquet ended at 8 p.m. When they returned to the hotel room, Jimmy walked over to A1-33. He couldn't speak out loud because his parents would hear him, but Jimmy wanted A1-33 to know how happy he was. He stared at his seat long and hard. All of a sudden, Jimmy heard a faint and familiar voice in his ear: "Jimmy, remember to have fun this week. You'll only get to play at Williamsport once."

Jimmy smiled and got ready for bed. He could hardly wait to play the next day.

CHAPTER 30

The week went by quickly. The US East team from Yonkers, New York won four straight games. The first game was a 4-1 victory over the US Midwest. Their second game was the closest of all, a narrow 2-1 win over Puerto Rico, in which Sharples pitched a great game. They were losing 1-0 in the bottom of the fifth, when Jimmy led off with a single, and Rockman blasted a shot over the left field fence for a two run homer.

After one day's rest, the US East destroyed US West by a score of 7-0. Barnes pitched brilliantly, and, as Sam said, "Everyone showed up to the ballpark with their hitting shoes on." During the semi-final game, the US East beat the US South 5-2. The only game left was the Little League Championship Game.

The US East team from Yonkers, New York was to face a team from Taiwan. The Taiwanese had not scored less than eight runs in a game. Further, they had not given up more than two runs a game throughout the whole tournament!

The US team was nervous. The game would be televised, and broadcast to millions of people across the world. Taiwan was a powerhouse, and the clear favorite.

Mr. Whitehill called for a meeting at the hotel, and everyone gathered into a private room at 7 p.m. The entire team was buzzing with excitement.

"Let's go," said Mr. Whitehill. "Everyone take a seat and quiet down."

Once everyone was in place, Mr. Whitehill smiled.

"There will be no speeches, no pep talks, and no concerns tonight," said the manager. "Instead, I have a big surprise. We have a visitor who all of you have heard of, and undoubtedly have seen before."

Jimmy moved forward to the edge of his seat, awaiting anxiously the next words to come out of Mr. Whitehill's mouth.

"This evening, boys, you're going to have the opportunity to meet one of the greatest baseball players of all time," said Mr. Whitehill.

The ballplayers began looking at each other with wonderment.

"Come on, Mr. Whitehill. Who is it?" yelled David.

"Okay, I'll tell you," said Mr. Whitehill. "Covering the game tomorrow as a special TV commentator is the one and only . . ."

Before Mr. Whitehill could say another word, the door of the room opened. Everyone quickly turned their heads around. There he was, just like he had appeared to Jimmy in his dream.

"I understand this is a New York team with a lot of talent and a lot of heart," said Mickey Mantle as he made his way to the front of the room.

Mr. Whitehill extended his arm, and the two men shook hands. Jimmy turned around to see what David's reaction to Mickey Mantle was. As he was focusing on Rockman, he noticed that the door to the meeting room was open. Standing in the hall, peering in with a smile, were Sam and Dad.

Jimmy knew that Sam somehow had something to do with Mickey Mantle visiting their team. Mr. Mantle sat down gently on a table that had been placed in front of the room.

"You know, the entire state of New York will be watching you," said Mr. Mantle.

The image of Mickey Mantle and Yogi Berra talking in the Yankee dugout came to Jimmy. He remembered that Mickey had said the same thing to Yogi. Jimmy remembered what Yogi had said back.

"The whole state, Mr. Mantle? I thought the whole country!" said Jimmy.

Everyone started to laugh, with the exception of Mr. Mantle. He walked slowly over to Jimmy and asked, "Do I know you, son?"

"No, sir. I don't think so," said Jimmy.

"You look very familiar," said Mickey.

Jimmy shrugged his shoulders at the Yankee great.

"What's your name?" Mickey asked.

"Jimmy McNeil," Jimmy answered.

"Well, Jimmy McNeil, you're right," said Mickey. "The entire country will be watching you tomorrow. How do you feel about that?"

"Nervous," Jimmy said.

"Well, let me share with you what my manager and good friend Yogi Berra once told me," said Mickey Mantle. "You've played very hard to get to this point. You're here because of your hard work, practice, and skill. You'll play well tomorrow, but not by worrying about it."

Jimmy smiled to himself. He had heard a speech like that before.

"Besides playing in the Little League World Championship, let me remind you of another important thing about being here in Pennsylvania," said Mickey. "What I'm talking about is friendship. To be a real ballplayer, you need to be a real team player. I want you all to support each other on and off the field. By doing so, you'll develop a friendship and a bond that will last long after the results of tomorrow's game are over."

Jimmy glanced around the room, watching the expressions on his teammates' faces. Barnes was the only one not listening intently. He was leaning back in his chair with his long legs sprawled out in front of him. His eyes stared downward at his own feet, as if Mickey Mantle's words bored him. Then Jimmy remembered that the legendary hero was speaking about teamwork on and off the field, something that meant nothing to Barnes.

After Mickey Mantle completed his talk, David and Jimmy went up to ask him for his autograph. Mr. Mantle obliged and other players went up for autographs too.

"Good luck tomorrow," Mickey Mantle said before leaving. Mr. Mantle then turned toward Jimmy. "You really look familiar. Are you sure we haven't met before?"

"No, Mr. Mantle," said Jimmy. "But I watched you on TV when I was much younger."

"Well, tomorrow, I get to watch you," said Mickey.

David and Jimmy thanked him for the autographs, and then exited the meeting room. Sam was waiting in the hallway.

"Quite a surprise, guys?" Sam asked.

"A great surprise!" Jimmy exclaimed.

"Hey, Sam, Mickey Mantle thinks he met Jimmy before," David said. Sam laughed and looked toward Jimmy.

"Well David, maybe he has," said Sam.

David looked at Jimmy strangely and shrugged.

"I think both of you should call it a night and get some sleep," said Sam. "You've got a big day tomorrow."

David and Jimmy agreed, and went back to their hotel rooms. Jimmy entered the room and told his mom and dad about the evening. Jillie had already fallen asleep. Jimmy knew it would be some time before he was ready to go to bed.

Mom insisted he needed the rest, though, and there was no arguing with her. Soon the lights were out, and everyone was trying to go to sleep.

Then, like a sudden flash, Jimmy found himself in a bright room. Across from him was Sam and to Sam's right was A1-33.

"You've come a long way in a very short period of time," said Sam. Jimmy nodded his head and listened.

"But there's much more for you to learn in the years ahead," said Sam. "Mickey Mantle spoke of friendship. This is the most valuable lesson you'll ever learn. Trust and loyalty takes more guts than hitting the winning run in the last inning. Do you understand, Jimmy?"

"Yes," Jimmy clearly responded.

"I'm proud to know you, Jimmy. Remember all that you've learned, and open your mind to learn more in the years ahead of you."

Jimmy found himself back in the hotel room. His eyes got heavy, and then shut. He fell into a deep slumber for the rest of the night.

CHAPTER 31

The grandstands were beginning to fill for the big game. From his practice position, Jimmy could see a group of men taking seats behind home plate. They were all carrying clipboards and stopwatches. Jimmy felt a nervous feeling come over him. Not only was he playing in the most important game of his life, but professional baseball scouts were watching too.

"Just have fun, Jimmy. Just have fun," he continued saying to himself.

Mr. Whitehill called everyone into the first base dugout. The team prepared for the introductions of the starting line-up. It would be announced over the ballpark's public address system. As they waited in the dugout for their names to be called, Mr. Whitehill paced back and forth.

"Remember what I told you last week," said their manager. "I want to see a 5-0 victory up on that scoreboard today."

The US team just nodded their heads quietly.

A reverberating voice from the speakers came belting out: "Representing the US East from Yonkers, New York: Manager, Harry Whitehill."

The crowd cheered as Mr. Whitehill walked out to home plate. The announcer's voice continued: "Leading off, and playing shortstop with a tournament batting average of .333, Jimmy McNeil."

Jimmy trotted out to Mr. Whitehill, who shook his hand and tapped him on the head. As the announcements continued, their team lined up one by one along the first base line. Once the announcer was done, the introduction of the Taiwanese team began. Jimmy could tell by the look on his opponents' faces that they were very serious about playing baseball.

When the announcements were completed, Mr. Whitehill kept the starting team by home plate. He handed the ball to Larry Barnes.

"You can do it, Larry. Now let's go out there and bring home the championship," said Mr. Whitehill.

Their manager extended his arm into the middle of the pack. All the players did the same, and in a ceremonious cheer, raised their arms forward in the air. The US East Team took their positions out in the field, and waited for the umpire to yell, "Play ball!"

The leadoff batter for Taiwan took his place in the batter's box. Barnes stepped onto the rubber. The umpire pointed to him, indicating for play to begin. As Jimmy crouched down in his fielding position, David Rockman began cheering for Barnes, and the entire team joined him. Barnes went into his wind up, and delivered the game's first pitch. He threw a blazing fastball and the Taiwanese batter watched the perfect pitch fly right by him.

Jimmy couldn't tell which sound was louder, the ball landing in the catcher's glove, or the wailing words of the umpire yelling, "Strike one!"

A thunderous cheer arose from the packed stadium crowd. Almost everybody there was cheering for the US team.

The McNeil family was sitting behind the first base dugout. Jimmy wished A1-33 was there to watch the game, positioned in the same location, as he would have been in Yankee Stadium, six rows back.

Barnes threw his second pitch. The Taiwanese batter began his swing and hit a line drive right over the head of José Sanchez at third. The ball was fair, and looked like it could fall in for extra bases. Danny Gutin in left field got to the ball quickly. Mr. Whitehill had drilled his team for this type of situation over and over again.

Jimmy went out to left field. He positioned himself between the second base bag and where the ball was fielded. He held up his arms indicating he was there to receive the cutoff throw. Danny threw the ball perfectly to him. Jimmy wheeled around with his arm cocked, ready to fire it to Kirby Bukowski, who was waiting at second base.

Jimmy saw that the runner had held up at first, though, and wasn't making an attempt to turn his hit into a double. Jimmy quickly ran the ball into the infield, staring at the base runner the entire time. He wanted it made very clear to the base runner that trying to move off first base would be a big mistake.

The group of Taiwanese fans cheered their leadoff batter's base hit. Jimmy delivered the ball to Barnes. He thought Barnes might need an encouraging word. As he placed the ball in his glove, Jimmy said, "It's okay, Larry. You can get the next three."

"You don't have to worry about it," said Barnes. "Just go back and play shortstop."

Jimmy thought Barnes's comments were discouraging, but he wasn't about to let anything throw him off today. He turned and hustled back to his position.

The next batter stepped up to the plate, and took the first pitch for a called strike. It seemed like the Taiwanese team was going to take the first pitch every time. Mr. Whitehill had used the same strategy against Larry Barnes during the league championship game.

Larry set himself on the mound and started his next wind up. The entire infield was set. On the next pitch the batter drilled a ground ball to Kirby at second base. Kirby charged in on the ball, cleanly scooped it, spun around quickly, and tossed the ball to Jimmy, who was covering second.

Jimmy scooped up the low throw, and in one motion, hopped off the base and shot the ball over to Rockman at first. David reached outward, extending his body as far as he could for the grab.

"Out!" hollered the umpire.

The US East team had turned an important double-play, and the crowd cheered loudly. It gave the team a needed boost of confidence, and sent a message to the Taiwanese team that they were up against tough competition.

The third batter took his spot at the plate, and to no one's surprise, he didn't swing at Barnes's first pitch. The count went to 1-1 before the hitter crushed a ball to center field. Bobby ran back deep, and as the ball began to dip, he lowered his body, throwing his arm forward toward the ball. Jimmy jumped into the air in celebration, as the ball landed in the web of Bobby's glove inches before hitting the ground.

Mr. Whitehill came out of the dugout cheering his team. The US East had pulled off two great defensive plays to end the top of the first inning.

"McNeil, Sharples, and Barnes. You're up!" yelled Coach Harrison.

Jimmy grabbed his bat and helmet and began practice swings in the on-deck circle. Chia Lee, the Taiwan pitcher, threw the fastest pitches Jimmy had ever seen.

"Keep calm," Jimmy mumbled to himself. " Remember all that you've learned."

The umpire looked toward Jimmy as he started his walk to home plate. Jimmy settled into the batter's box and looked to Mr. Whitehill for instructions. He flashed Jimmy the take sign. Jimmy nodded that he understood the signal, and prepared to wait for the first pitch. Chia started his wind up and delivered a fastball that moved as quick as Jimmy had ever seen.

"Strike one," yelled the umpire.

Gripping his bat, Jimmy dug into the batter's box. If I could get a base hit right now, I could lift the team up for a first inning rally, Jimmy thought.

Chia Lee stood on the mound tall and strong. He was definitely the toughest pitching opponent Jimmy had ever come across. He wound up and released a ball that appeared to be going into the strike zone. Jimmy began his swing, but the ball was moving so fast he could barely get his bat around in time. Jimmy made slight contact, and the ball skipped past the catcher for a foul tip and strike two.

It was 0-2, and Jimmy stepped out of the batter's box. He took a deep breath and looked toward Mr. Whitehill, who was encouraging him to swing at a good pitch. As soon as Jimmy was set back into the box, the pitcher went into his wind up. Jimmy was geared up for a fastball. Once the ball was released from the pitcher's hand, Jimmy's bat came off his shoulders.

As he was swinging, his heart fell into his stomach. The Taiwanese ace had taken all the speed off the pitch. Jimmy's swing was finished before the ball reached home plate.

"Strike three!" yelled the ump.

Jimmy had been fooled by a change up. With his head down, he walked past Sharples and headed into the dugout. Pro scouts, Mickey Mantle, TV, the press, and I just looked like a fool in front of all of America, thought Jimmy. The dugout was quiet as he took his seat and watched Bobby Sharples take his turn at the plate.

After the first called strike, Mr. Whitehill flashed Bobby the bunt sign. He wanted to test the Taiwanese infield. As the pitch was thrown, Bobby squared around and bunted between the pitcher and the third baseman.

"Go hard, Bobby. Go hard!" yelled Mr. Harrison, who was coaching first.

Chia scooped up the ball quickly and threw a bullet to his first baseman. The ball beat Bobby by at least three steps for the second out.

Larry Barnes went up to the plate. Mr. Whitehill was trying to give him the take sign, but Barnes wasn't paying attention. Before Mr. Whitehill could call time out, the pitcher was throwing. The ball was moving high to the outside, but Barnes swung anyway. His big bat hit under the ball and sent it straight up into the air. The Taiwanese pitcher called for the ball and secured it firmly in his glove for the third and final out.

Mr. Whitehill ran across the infield to the dugout, clapping his hands.

"It's okay, boys," said the manager. "We have plenty of other chances. Everyone keep your heads up, and let's play tough ball!"

Mr. Whitehill kept Larry in the dugout. From the field, no one could hear what he was saying. Jimmy was sure Mr. Whitehill was upset that Larry hadn't taken a pitch as instructed.

The top half of the second inning brought up Chia Lee as the inning's lead off hitter. The count went to 2-1. Barnes went into his wind up and fired a fastball, which Lee swung around on and connected. The ball went into deep left field and bounced about five feet before the fence. The bounce carried the ball up and over the fence, and the umpire yelled for a ground-rule double.

Taiwan's star pitcher and hitter went into second base. Jimmy and Chia's eyes met. Chia gave Jimmy a smile and tipped his helmet to him. Jimmy was taken back by this familiar gesture, and tipped his cap back, smiling in return. Jimmy then looked toward the mound as Barnes got a new ball from the umpire and prepared to face Taiwan's number five batter.

Larry seemed in control as he delivered two consecutive strikes to start off. On the third fastball, though, the batter connected for a long and deep hit. Jimmy didn't have to turn around to know it was a home run.

Taiwan took a 2-0 lead. Mr. Whitehill called time out and took a walk out to the pitcher's mound to speak with Larry. Larry walked around nervously, staring at the ground. Jimmy looked up at the camera crews that seemed to be catching Larry's reaction on TV, and felt bad for him. He knew how easily Larry got shook up. If Mr. Whitehill didn't help him collect his composure, the US Team would be in trouble.

Bobby Sharples had pitched the last game, and according to tournament rules, a pitcher couldn't pitch two consecutive games. After a small conversation, the umpire encouraged Mr. Whitehill to return to the dugout.

Larry Barnes faced another five hitters before he struck out a batter to end the inning. With good defense and communication, the US East managed to hold Taiwan scoreless for the remaining half of the inning.

The next four innings did not go well for the US East Team. David Rockman got a base hit in the bottom of the second, but otherwise, the team went completely hitless. In the top of the fourth, Taiwan added three more runs, which included a solo homer by Chia Lee.

As the US Team entered the dugout in the bottom half of the sixth inning, Mr. Whitehill sat everyone down on the bench.

"Eight days ago, we all stood by home plate and I told you that I wanted to see the scoreboard read US East 5 Opponent 0," said Mr. Whitehill. "Now, here it is a week later, and we're losing 5-0. We have one last chance. Forget the TV cameras, forget the World Championship, and think about yourselves."

David and Jimmy looked at each other. Jimmy knew that this was serious, and it would take a lot for the US East team to win.

"You've played hard all summer to get to this point. Each and every one of you is as good as every player on the Taiwan team," said the manager. "It's not a matter of playing hard, but playing smart. Lee is still throwing heat. I want everyone taking two steps back in the batter's box to give you more time. We need to help them make mistakes. Every batter is to take two strikes before you have the green light to swing. Look for signs."

Two strikes, thought Jimmy, we've never taken two before! Jimmy was intrigued by this new strategy.

"We have to make things happen," said the manager. "You know that everyone's very proud of you. Now, I want you to win this game, in this inning, for yourselves. Zachary Gutin is the leadoff hitter, then McNeil, Sharples, and the rest of the team. Let's go get them."

Mr. Whitehill ran out to the coach's box. The team was pumped up. Zachary went to home plate, and Jimmy headed to the on-deck circle.

Gutin did exactly what Mr. Whitehill had said. He stepped back in the box and waited for the Taiwanese pitcher to step on the rubber.

Chia Lee seemed perplexed as to why Zachary was standing so far back in the box. He went into his wind up and threw his first pitch, which bounced off the middle of the plate for ball one. Mr. Whitehill clapped and encouraged Zachary. Little by little, the cheering increased from the quiet and somewhat somber US fans. The next pitch was thrown high for ball two.

The Taiwanese pitcher stood confidently on the mound and fired a fastball for a called strike one. The next pitch came in low and to the inside for ball three. Lee now seemed a bit nervous. Zachary was in the back of the box and watched as the Taiwanese pitcher threw the ball high and outside for ball four.

"Batter, take your base!" yelled the umpire as Zachary trotted down to first.

Jimmy began his walk to home plate. It seemed like the walk lasted forever. On the way to the plate, Jimmy looked up at the press box. He could see all the sports casters sitting with Mickey Mantle. Mr. Mantle leaned back from his microphone, and looked toward Jimmy. He raised his hands with his thumb up in the air.

Jimmy reached the batter's box and stepped deep into it as Mr. Whitehill had instructed. Even though the team was down 5-0, Jimmy felt like they were still in the game. Lee took his position on the mound, and Jimmy set himself in the box, waiting for the delivery. He could hear Mr. Whitehill encouraging him from the third base coach's box. From the dugout, Jimmy could hear his team starting to chatter.

Lee fired the ball. As it made its way quickly toward home plate, Jimmy could see that it was going to be a perfect strike.

Jimmy had the pitch timed perfectly in his mind. His eyes followed it all the way, and he knew he could make contact when he had his chance. Jimmy turned to Mr. Whitehill, who surprisingly signaled for Jimmy to swing away.

"Stay back in the box, and make sure it's a good pitch," shouted Mr. Whitehill.

Jimmy nodded and positioned himself at home plate. He looked up into the stands above the first base dugout. There were the people that were most important in his life: Mom, Dad, Jillie, and his very special friend, Sam. Jimmy could see that they were all staring at him, giving him a sense of support.

Mom was clasping her hands together and holding them in front of her. Dad was pretending he was swinging a bat, encouraging Jimmy to get a hit. Jillie smiled warmly and held up her hand, her fingers curled outward as she waved to him. Then Jimmy's eyes met Sam's. Sam had taken his index finger from his right hand and pointed it to his forehead. With two fingers, he grasped the beak of his hat and tipped it to Jimmy.

"Remember all that you've learned," Jimmy said to himself.

Every lesson that A1-33 had shown him over the past few months seemed to rush before his eyes. Then, like a movie reel slowing down, Jimmy saw Lou Gehrig instructing him in batting practice. Jimmy looked up at Sam and tipped the beak of his helmet. The usual smile grew over Sam's face as he nodded back.

Jimmy dug his back foot into the dirt and held his bat off of his shoulder. He separated his feet and prepared himself for the pitch.

Think smart, Jimmy thought as the wind-up started. In the first inning he threw two straight fastballs. He's going to do the same.

The Taiwanese pitcher released the ball. Jimmy's eyes locked on it. The ball was coming straight down the middle and Jimmy was able to time it perfectly. His left arm guided his swing as the bat came off his shoulder.

Jimmy smashed a line drive over the second baseman's head into right field. With his head forward, he sprinted down the first base line. Mr. Harrison was directing Zachary to run to second, which he did quickly. By the time the right fielder came up with the ball, Zach was at second and Jimmy had reached first base. It was first and second with no outs. The stadium fans were now up on their feet.

"Way to hit that ball, Jimmy," called Mr. Harrison.

"Thanks," Jimmy said, as he stood on first trying to catch his breath.

Bobby Sharples came up to the plate and took two balls before Chia delivered a strike. It seemed that the Taiwanese ace was beginning to tire. Mr. Whitehill signaled the bunt sign to Bobby.

Lee wound up, and Bobby squared around for a sacrifice bunt. The pitch came in waist high, and Bobby directed the ball perfectly between the pitcher and the first baseman. Zachary took off for third, and Jimmy's wheels moved as fast as they could as he headed for second.

The Taiwanese pitcher came up with the ball. He turned to third to see if he could get a force out on Gutin, but then he spun the other way and fired the ball to second, for the sure out. The shortstop was maneuvering to cover second.

Jimmy could see that they were going to make an attempt to get him. His feet launched off the ground like he was pushing off of a diving board. With his arms extended, Jimmy reached for second base. As he landed on the ground, he could hear the umpire yell, "Safe!"

Jimmy looked up from the bag to see what was happening, and saw Sharples crossing first base safely. The shortstop was standing next to Jimmy with the ball in his hand. Jimmy quickly called time out.

Everyone in the ballpark was going crazy. It seemed like there was a lot of action in the press box. The bases were loaded with no outs, and the two strongest hitters on the US East Team were coming up to bat. Mr. Whitehill was as excited as he could possibly be from the third base coach's box. Larry Barnes made his way up to the plate.

"Follow instructions, Larry," yelled Mr. Whitehill.

Barnes didn't respond. He just looked straight ahead at Chia Lee, who was now nervously walking back and forth on the mound. The first three pitches to Barnes weren't even near the plate. On each pitch, Jimmy could swear he thought Larry was going to swing. He remembered back to the league championship, when Rockman had made him lose control.

Larry does his own thing, Jimmy thought to himself. If he walks, one run would come in and then David Rockman would represent the tying run.

Lee delivered the ball and, from Jimmy's view on second base, it looked as if it was going to be way outside. Like a nightmare coming true, Barnes started to swing. As the bat came whipping around, Barnes realized the ball wasn't even near the strike zone. He tried to pull back his swing, but it appeared he had gone too far.

"Strike one," yelled the umpire.

"No way," shouted Barnes. "I held back. It's ball four."

"Sorry, son. You swung."

"You're blind," hollered Barnes. "I should be on first base."

The home plate umpire slowly lifted the mask off his face, stepped around the batter's box, and said as loud as he could, "You're out of the game!"

Barnes stood there with his mouth open. Mr. Whitehill came running over, tapped Larry on the helmet, and walked him into the dugout. As they got closer, Larry took off his helmet and threw it as hard as he could against the dugout wall.

Mr. Whitehill brought Marc Dunlop in to hit for Barnes. He would have to continue with the existing 3-1 count. Jimmy looked up into the stands while Marc was taking his practice swings. The contingency of scouts were talking to each other and shaking their heads. Jimmy saw one take a pencil and make a crossing out motion on his clipboard.

The umpire pointed to Lee to resume pitching, and the game was back underway. From second base, Jimmy watched as Marc was clearly overpowered by two fastballs right down the middle. He never had a chance coming in cold from the bench, Jimmy thought. There was now one out, but still time.

David Rockman over the last few months had become Jimmy's best friend. He was also the best teammate he had ever had. David took strides of determination as he made his way from the on-deck circle to home plate. David then stepped deep into the batter's box, and prepared himself to take pitches until there was a called strike.

The Taiwan team realized the US strategy and fired the first pitch past David for a called strike one. David didn't even flinch. He stayed completely in place while the catcher threw the ball back to the mound. Chia Lee then looked at David strangely. David was like a statute. Jimmy knew that David was up to something, but only David knew what it was.

The pitcher threw his next pitch, a fastball right down the middle. David stood still and just let the ball blow by him. The count went to 0-2, and the entire stadium fell to a hush.

As Lee settled himself back on the mound, he began to smile, almost with a sense of overconfidence. He stepped up to the rubber and grabbed the ball tight in his hand. He went into his wind up, and Jimmy saw David start to smirk. The Taiwanese pitcher kicked his leg forward and released the ball. He had thrown a change up, the very same one he threw to Jimmy in the first inning.

David didn't miss a trick. Jimmy believed David knew it was coming. David had timed his swing perfectly, and "rocked the ball like the rock of ages" deep into left field. Every head in the stadium moved with the flight of the ball as it cleared the fence for a grand slam home run.

After Jimmy scored, he waited for David at home plate, watching him touch all the bases. Jimmy felt so proud this was his best friend. They celebrated the home run with gusto, but realized they were down one run and the bases were clear.

David and Jimmy stood at the fence of the dugout and watched the Taiwanese team change pitchers. Mike Laffey was up next. David started to cheer for him as he took his warm up swings. Everyone joined in, all except Barnes that is, who sat on a corner of the bench and stared at the ground.

Jimmy couldn't help thinking that if Barnes had only followed Mr. Whitehill's signs, he would have been walked. A run would have scored, and chances were that the game would have been tied at five all.

The count went to 2-2 on Mike. On the next pitch, Mike hit a chopper to third. The Taiwanese infielder made a clean play and threw him out for out number two.

The US East Team's last hope at the plate was José Sanchez, whose All-Star batting average was only .167. Jimmy continued to cheer with all the energy he had left. José swung at the second pitch and hit a high pop up to second. As Jimmy watched the ball dropping from the sky, all his hopes of winning the Little League World Series began falling with it.

The second baseman closed his glove on the ball, and the game was over.

The Taiwanese team poured onto the field and the umpire signaled that the game had ended. Cheering and celebrating on the field would go on for some time. Jimmy was happy for the Taiwanese players, but he was really upset he had lost. Jimmy turned to his best-friend David in the dugout.

"It was a great series, wasn't it?" asked David.

"Yeah," said Jimmy. "And it sure was fun."

CHAPTER 32

Jim was curious as to why Coach Sandine had called him. Earlier, he had received a message at his college dormitory to be at the coach's office at precisely 2 p.m. The large clock on the wall read 2:20. Jim could hear two voices from behind the closed door, but only Coach Sandine's was recognizable.

As Jim continued to wait for his college coach, he thought back over his last four years at Arizona State University. They'd played 80 games a season, and qualified for the NCAA College Tournament each year. He knew he was fortunate to have made the starting team as a freshman. It had given him great experience.

Jim had a lot of respect for Coach Sandine. Coach had taught him a lot over the last four years.

It had been almost eleven years since Jim's Dad had brought home A1-33. That night seemed like yesterday, and so much had happened since then. Through the years, A1-33 had taken him back to Yankee Stadium for visits with the great legends of the game.

Jimmy had learned everything from hitting to the opposite field, to using his power to place them over the fence, a skill that he thought was only for big guys, like David Rockman. The thought of the big guy brought a smile to Jim's face.

David and Jim had remained best friends since their last year in Little League. They were co-captains together on the high school baseball team. David's true love of football had earned him a full scholarship to Penn State, where he was selected as an All-American linebacker two years in a row. Jim's buddy was going to play pro football, and he was the first round draft choice of the New York Giants.

That last year in Little League bonded Jim with another individual, a true friend whom he had really missed. Jim hadn't seen Sam since they dropped him off at the train station, the day they got back from Williamsport. Sam had turned to Jim and said, "See you at the stadium."

No one had seen or heard from Sam since.

Jim had worried about him for the longest time, and searched everywhere he could think of. He would hang out at Yankee Stadium after it reopened in 1976, believing Sam would show up to a game. Jim even went to Pop's Candy Store hoping he would find him there. But to Jim's surprise, it had become a bookstore.

Jim went to the New York City Office of Records, trying to find out who owned Pop's. He thought this would lead him to Sam. The clerk at the city office told him Pop's closed down in 1945. Jim never bothered to try to figure that out or discuss it with anyone. Who would believe him?

Yankee dreams, a mysterious baseball glove he received as a Christmas present, conversations with Sam at Pop's Candy Store thirty years after it had closed down. The more Jim thought about it all, the more it didn't make sense. It didn't matter anyway. Jim knew Sam was much more than Sam had ever told him.

Even though things had been great for Jim, they hadn't been great for everyone. Larry Barnes had given up on sports after the Little League World Series. Everyone said it was a shame, since Larry was so talented. Jim didn't know what he was doing these days. He heard that Larry was working part-time for a moving company.

Jim looked back up at the clock, which now read 2:25. The voices from within his coach's office had quieted. Jim then saw the doorknob on Coach Sandine's office turn as the door opened. Coach Sandine gestured for Jim to enter the office.

"Jim, I'd like to introduce you to Mr. Tansey," said Coach Sandine.

Jim extended his arm out as he shook hands, all the time wondering whom he was meeting.

"Jim, I'm a scout with the New York Yankees," announced Mr. Tansey. "How would you feel spending the summer in pinstripes, playing in an instructional league?"

Jim's face lit up before he could even answer.

"It doesn't pay a lot, but you become part of the club," continued the scout. "It provides you the opportunity to move up next season to a higher class of minor league ball."

"Yes, yes, Mr. Tansey," Jim said. "I really want to play, but I'd like to discuss it with my parents first."

"Absolutely," Mr. Tansey responded. "But we'd like you to report to Fort Lauderdale, Florida a week after graduation."

"Thank you sir. I'll call my parents today."

"Good," Mr. Tansey said. "Here's my card, and be sure to contact me as soon as you can. There are a lot of ballplayers who'd like the opportunity if you don't."

"Oh, but I do sir," promised Jim.

Coach Sandine winked at Jim. Jim then turned to leave, and nervously stumbled over a chair that was in the coach's office. He heard laughter erupt behind him as he made his way out the door. Jim eyed a pay phone down the hall. He picked up the pace as quickly as he could. When he got to the phone, Jim misdialed three times before he made a connection.

Jim could tell by the excitement in his parents' voices, that they supported his decision to play baseball in Florida.

CHAPTER 33

Leaving the bedroom Jim had grown in was especially tough. In recent years, Jim had stood in front of A1-33 many times with a packed bag at his side, always telling him that he wished he could bring him along. A1-33's numeric plate seemed to shine as if he always understood.

But today was very different.

It wasn't different because Jim was leaving to play ball with the Yankees, but because his mother and father had sold the house, and were moving into an apartment. Jillie would be attending college in September, and they felt their home would be too big for just the two of them. A1-33 would be transported to their new home until Jim eventually had a place of his own in Fort Lauderdale.

Mom and Dad were waiting for their son in the car. As they pulled out of the driveway in route to the airport, Jim looked up at his room. He could barely see A1-33 through the window.

Suddenly, Jim felt a sick feeling come over him. He looked straight ahead through the car window as they continued down the road. He felt something was very wrong.

John could see the moving truck through the living room window. He walked to the front door and looked surprised as he slowly swung it open.

"Hi, Mr. McNeil," said Larry Barnes.

"Well hello, Larry," said John. "What brings you here?"

"I work with these gorillas," Larry said, pointing to the moving crew standing behind him.

"Well, come in guys. We have twenty-five years worth of household goods that need to be loaded."

The movers worked for hours, clearing each room one at a time. They eventually made their way upstairs, and then separated into different bedrooms. Larry entered into Jim's room. He looked at everything that had been collected over the years.

Barnes became envious as he read the articles about Jim's high school and college accomplishments. Jim's mother had framed each one, and displayed them on the walls. Larry threw them down onto the bed.

He turned toward the window and spotted A1-33. A sinister smile came across his face as he walked up to the seat. He thought back to Williamsport, when Jim had taken A1-33 out of his hands.

"Little weasel," Larry said under his breath.

He then looked over his shoulder to see if anyone was around. When he was sure he was all by himself, Larry picked up A1-33 and carried it outside. He quickly went to the other side of the truck where no one could see him.

Locating a group of bushes across the street, Larry tossed A1-33 behind them. He would come back later to retrieve the stadium seat when no one was around. I should be able to get at least 200 dollars for this hunk of junk, Larry thought. After all, big shot McNeil doesn't need any more luck.

Later that evening, Larry Barnes drove his car down the street, and stopped in front of the bushes where he had hidden A1-33 earlier. Using both arms, he pulled back the branches and grabbed A1-33 off the ground, lifting it through a bush. Once it had cleared, Barnes placed the seat in the trunk of his car, slammed it tight, and laughed as he climbed behind the wheel.

Larry drove directly to a pawnshop. He carried A1-33 in, and placed it on the counter. A grumpy attendant, chewing on the end of a cigar, slowly made his way over to Larry Barnes from the other side of the store.

"What you got?" he asked.

"Prime Yankee memorabilia," Barnes responded.

The clerk took the cigar out of his mouth, and placed it in a dirty ashtray.

"What do you mean, prime Yankee memorabilia?" he asked.

Barnes explained that this might be the only original Yankee seat not destroyed during the renovation eleven years earlier. The pawn shop attendant picked up A1-33 and examined it closely.

"I'll give you twenty-five dollars for it," said the pawn shop attendant.

"Are you crazy? I want $200 bucks," said Barnes.

"Forget it," responded the attendant. "Get out of here."

"Okay," said Barnes. "I just want to get rid of this thing quickly. Give me $100."

The pawn shop attendant looked up slowly. He picked up the cigar in his hand, and used it as a pointing tool.

"I'm going to give you $50 bucks," said the attendant. "Take it or leave it!

"Uh, just give me the money," said Barnes. "I'm out of here."

As Barnes left the pawnshop, A1-33 was put on the tile floor, and then kicked along the counter by the shop attendant. It finally came to a stop in the corner facing a counter filled with old radios, tape recorders, and 8-track players.

Jim began tossing and turning in bed. He was having a nightmare. In his dream, Jim could see a dark room with the silhouette of a glass counter. In the counter were all types of items, but it wasn't clear to Jim what they were. Suddenly he heard the familiar voice he had heard in so many of his dreams.

"Help, Jim! I need your help," cried the voice.

Jim suddenly sat up in his bed.

What a strange dream, he thought. Jim felt the sweat dripping from his forehead. He got up and walked into the living room, and then sat down on the couch. Jim stared straight ahead. Something felt very wrong, and he didn't know why.

CHAPTER 34

How old would you be if you didn't know how old you were?

–Satchel Paige

Playing in the Instructional League was going great for Jim. He was playing shortstop, and had a batting average of .395. He had even put four over the fence in the last sixteen games. The caliber of ball was good, and all the guys on the team were serious about a career in professional baseball.

Jim's goal was to keep up the pace, and hopefully be retained as a minor league player the following season.

On this day, practice was a light workout. Coach Winslow wanted to give all the pitchers a rest. The team took batting practice with the pitching machine. This was just fine with Jim, since he was tired. He didn't get much sleep the night before, and he was concerned as to why A1-33 had been calling to him in his nightmare.

Jim knew something wasn't right. He headed into the locker room to shower and change. He figured he would take it easy for the rest of the day.

It was October, and there were only six games left. As Jim was getting changed, he thought it would feel good to get home and see his parents. He even wanted to swing by Jillie's college and spend the day with her.

David Rockman made the training camp cut and was now with the New York Giants on the professional roster. Jim wanted to go to the stadium in New Jersey and see a game as well.

He walked to the ball field parking lot with his teammate, Tommy Taylor. "Do you need a ride back to the apartment?" Tommy asked.

Jim was just about to say yes, when the words got stuck in his throat. "I don't believe it," Jim answered.

"What don't you believe?" asked Tommy.

"Nothing," said Jim. "Why don't you head back without me."

Jim's eyes were fixed straight ahead. There he was, sitting on a bench adjacent to the parking lot. Jim returned to the last image he had seen of him. He hadn't changed. He was even wearing the same clothes, and of course, his old Yankee hat.

"Jim," Sam said with a concerned look on his face. "How are you?"

"I looked for you for so long," said Jim.

"I know, Jim."

"What happened to you? Where have you been?"

"There's a lot for us to talk about," said Sam, "and I'll explain what I can while we travel."

"Travel?" Jim asked.

Sam looked very serious. Jim moved closer so he could hear Sam better.

"We need to go back to New York," Sam said. "A1-33 has been stolen."

"I knew something was wrong last night in my dream," said Jim.

"I know," Sam interrupted, "when your mom and dad moved yesterday, Larry Barnes was on the crew that moved them from the house. He grabbed A1-33, and I can't tell for sure what he did with him."

Jim's heart dropped. He hoped A1-33 was all right.

"I do know that together we can cover more ground," said Sam. "We need to leave for New York right away. I have us booked on a flight in one hour, and that doesn't give us much time."

"Okay, let me tell the coach I have a family emergency and I need to go home," said Jim. "I'll be right back."

Jim ran back into the locker room and explained to his coach he had to fly back home immediately. Jim apologized and hoped he would be able to return shortly.

"Look, Jim, family's important. If it's necessary for you to go, do it, and hustle back," said Jim's coach. "I don't want to lose my number one hitter, and the best infielder I've ever seen."

"Thanks coach," said Jim.

With his gym bag in hand, Jim ran back out to the parking lot where Sam had a cab waiting. "Jump in, Jim," said Sam, "You and I have a lot of catching up to do."

"Where have you been all these years?" Jim asked. "You just disappeared without a word, not even a trace. I tried to find you for the longest time."

Sam looked toward Jim and smiled gently.

"I was working," said Sam.

"Working? Working where?" asked Jim. "I went to Yankee Stadium time and time again. No one had seen you. Everyone expected you to be at the reopening of the stadium."

"I work in many different places and at many different times," Sam said. "I have a job few understand or would believe."

"What type of job? You can tell me," pleaded Jim. "I trust you, and I've always believed you."

Sam looked down for a moment. When he looked up, his eyes seemed as soft and sincere as they ever had before.

"Yes, you always have, Jim, and I appreciate that," said Sam. "I travel to wherever I'm needed. I help those individuals who come close to doing something great, but just need a little guidance. You see Jim, I'm what you call a 'Guardian of Hopes and Dreams.'"

Sam looked at Jim and smiled. Jim's mouth slowly began to open as he struggled to get out the words.

"Ever since Dad brought home A1-33, so many things have happened," sputtered Jim. "Is it all magic, is that what you're telling me?"

"No," continued Sam. "It's all just a natural progression of events, driven by destiny. My job is to make sure things stay on track. It's individuals like you that make things happen."

"Why? Why must they happen?" asked Jim.

"Because it leads to creating something wonderful," explained Sam. "Sometimes it's for only a handful of people, other times it's for millions."

Jim was astonished. He couldn't believe what he was hearing.

"So who else have you helped?" Jim asked in bewilderment.

"So many other people it would take an eternity to tell you," said Sam with a smile.

"Does anyone ever help you," Jim asked.

Sam smiled, and they stepped out of the cab.

Sam and Jim's flight to New York City was filled with talk about A1-33 and their plan to save him. When they arrived in New York, Jim called his parents' new home to let them know he had flown into town.

"Why did you fly back?" Dad asked, sounding worried. "Is everything okay?"

"We have a friend who needs some help," Jim answered.

"Who? It must be serious for you to leave the ball club. Do you need my help?"

"Yes," said Jim. "Can you meet Sam and I at Yankee Stadium?"

"Did you say Sam?" Dad asked.

"Just meet us by the players' entrance in an hour, I'll explain everything then."

Jim hung up the phone and he and Sam immediately went to work.

Exactly one hour later, Sam and Jim were standing in front of the players' entrance at Yankee Stadium. There was a lot of activity going on, since the Yankees were playing that evening in game five of the American League Championship Playoff.

Jimmy's father drove up and got out of his car. He looked at Sam, but was speechless.

"Hi, Mac," Sam said.

Mac smiled and extended his hand out firmly, shaking Sam's hand. He then looked at Jim and hugged him.

"It's great to see the both of you together again," said Dad. "I don't know why we're here, but I'm glad we are."

Sam grinned and brought Jimmy's father up to date with what was going on. Within moments, all three men were at the corner of 161st and Jerome Avenue. Sam opened the door, and Mac and Jim entered Pop's Candy Store.

CHAPTER 35

Jim's visit to Pop's Candy Store ten years earlier raced through his mind. The store looked exactly the same. Behind the counter, and wearing the same apron, was Pop.

"Hi, Sam," Pop said.

"Hi, Pop," Sam returned.

"The kid has grown up."

"He sure has."

"Has his dream come true yet?" Pop asked.

"Not yet, Pop," said Sam. "But he's working on it."

Jim's father's head turned back and forth from Pop to Sam, like he was watching a tennis match.

Suddenly things were starting to fall into place. Sam had said in the cab earlier that he was in many places at many different times. Jim didn't need to ask any more questions.

As if Sam had heard his thoughts, he looked at Jim.

"No, I do not travel time," Sam said. "Time travels to me."

Listening to Sam, Jim's dad collapsed into the seat. What Sam was telling him kept getting more and more incredible!

"Look around you. It's 1985, and this store was here over forty years ago," said Sam. "It's still here, Jim. You see, time passes, but it never goes away."

"What about A1-33? Can he go through time as well?" Jim asked.

"No, A1-33 is special," explained Sam. "His abilities were created by the love of a game and the people who surround it. This is why we must not let A1-33 be destroyed."

By this time, Dad was holding his head with a shocked expression on his face. Then, as if he had just woken from a nap, he jumped up.

"A1-33 will not be destroyed," Dad shouted. "I didn't let it happen in 1974, and I won't let it happen now."

Jim and his Dad then high-fived and finalized their plan. Sam explained to Jim's father that last night Jim had envisioned A1-33 in a dark corner, near a glass counter filled with everything from jewelry to electronics.

"Well that's a pawn shop," announced Dad.

"That's what I think," said Sam. "Now let's think. Larry Barnes wouldn't have sold A1-33 too close to home because someone may have known that it belonged to Jim. But I don't believe he would've gone too far, because he wouldn't want to hold on to it too long."

"Let's take the yellow pages and divide the shops between the three of us." Jim said. "We'll cover more ground this way."

They did as Jim suggested, and got down to work. There were eighteen pawn shops in all. It was now eight o'clock, and they had agreed to return back to Pop's at exactly ten p.m.

As they all got up to leave, Jim wondered if the store would go away and then come back. He turned to Pop.

"Will you be here two hours from now?" Jim asked Pop.

"Jim, I've got nowhere to go," he responded. "I have all the time in the world."

The two hours passed by quickly. Jim asked the same question in every shop he entered: "Do you have an old Yankee Stadium seat?"

The answer was always no.

Jim was hoping that either his dad or Sam had enjoyed better luck. His watch read exactly ten o'clock as he walked back into Pop's. The minute Jim saw the look on Sam, his father, and Pop, he knew they hadn't had any luck either.

"Nothing?" Jim asked.

Everyone remained silent.

Suddenly, Jim began to receive flash images. They were occurring so quickly, he had difficulty recognizing what they were. He dropped into a seat. His dad came over to him quickly. It seemed like Jim was getting sick.

"He's okay, Mac. Let him be," said Sam. "Concentrate, Jim. What is it you see?"

"It's a neon sign that reads, 'Clams All You Can Eat,'" said Jim.

"What else?"

"It's a movie theater."

"What's playing?"

"Nothing. It must be closed down, because there's nothing on the marquee."

All of a sudden, Jim's father jumped out of his seat.

"That's the old River Theater north of Untermyer Park!" shouted Dad. "It's right next to Joe's Clam House. Come on, let's go."

They ran out of the store and jumped into the car as fast as they could. As Jim looked back at Pop's, the storefront slowly changed into a bookstore. Jim smiled to himself. Pop hasn't gone away for good, he thought. He'll be back.

John McNeil's car raced along the Saw Mill River Parkway. He pulled off the Odell Ave. exit and made a left toward the river. Up ahead, they could see the movie marquee.

"There it is!" John yelled as he pointed across the street from the theater.

Sam and Jim both looked left and saw Duke's Pawnshop. In front of the store, there was a sloppy looking man who was locking the door and turning to walk away. Jim was out of the car before it even stopped. His father screeched the brakes.

"Hey you!" Jim yelled as he ran toward the man.

The man appeared to get frightened, and he backed up against the window of the store.

"I don't have any money," the shopkeeper yelled.

At this point, Sam and Mac were out of the car and crossing the street.

"Money? Oh, I don't want your money," said Jim. "It's just that you have A1-33 inside."

"What are you talking about?" asked the man quizzically.

"A1-33," Jim insisted. "My Yankee Stadium seat."

"Oh, you mean *my* stadium seat," the man returned.

"It's my seat, and it was stolen," Jim interjected.

"Hey, I don't know where it came from," the pawn shop attendant said plainly. "It didn't have any names on it. I paid cash for it and, unless you want to buy it, it belongs to me."

John and Sam were now standing next to Jim.

"How much do you want for it?" Jim's father asked.

"200 dollars," the man returned coldly.

"200 dollars!" Jim exclaimed. "Don't try to rip us off."

"That will be fine," said Jim's father. "Just open up the door and give it to us."

A sinister smile appeared on the man's unshaven face as he unlocked the door and let them in. John McNeil opened up his wallet and took out a credit card and placed in on the counter.

"Where's A1-33?" Jim said strongly.

"The seat's in the corner, hot shot," said the attendant. "You can have it once I finish the transaction."

Jim's eyes quickly scanned the shop until they fixed on A1-33. Jim ran to him as if he were stealing second base. His arms extended forward as he got closer. Jim's hands opened up and grasped A1-33 by the armrest.

Jim felt a strange sensation go through him, as if he was becoming permanently bonded to A1-33. Holding up his stadium seat, he turned and looked toward his dad and Sam. Jim looked down at his old box seat.

"Sorry, buddy," Jimmy said. "This should never have happened to you. I promise it will never, ever happen again."

Then Jim, Sam and Dad walked slowly with A1-33 across the street and climbed into the car.

"Let's head home," Dad said.

"Drop me off at the train station, would you please?" asked Sam.

"Sam, you can't leave," pleaded Jim. "Mom would love to see you. Please come back to the house."

"I can't, Jim. I've got work to do," Sam explained, and then turned and stared straight ahead.

Jim's father drove to the station. As they approached the stop, Jim touched Sam on the shoulder.

"Sam, when will I see you again?" Jim asked.

"Sooner than you think," he answered.

Jimmy's father drove home quickly, and as he pulled into the driveway of their new apartment, Jim saw his mom standing outside in the parking lot. She came running over to the car. Jim opened up the door, and she jumped in and gave him a hug so hard he thought his neck would break.

"Hey, Mom!" Jim exclaimed.

Before he could go any further, she interrupted, "I've been so worried about you. Where have you been?"

Jim made an attempt to explain, but his Mom continued talking.

"You got a phone call about an hour ago from your baseball coach in Florida," said Mom.

"What did he say?" asked Jim.

"I told him that you'd be returning to Florida shortly, but he said not to come back."

"That's crazy," Dad said. "Are they nuts? Why would they tell Jim not to come back?"

Mom's face slowly grew a smile.

"Didn't you two listen to the Yankee game tonight?" Mom asked. "The Yankees won the American League Championship."

Jim and his Dad looked at each other.

"We were so busy we forgot all about it," Jim said.

"Well, the second baseman for the Yankees broke his leg sliding," Mom said. "Jim, the Yankees are going to the World Series, and they want you to be on the roster immediately—to play second base!"

Through the excitement in his mom's voice, the words began to slowly sink in.

"Jim, are you listening to me?" Mom asked. "You have to report to the Yankee Stadium office at 8 a.m. tomorrow morning to sign a major league contract."

CHAPTER 36

Jim and his parents entered the administrative offices at exactly 8 a.m. The receptionist sitting at the desk looked up.

"Are you Jim McNeil?'" she asked.

"Yes," Jim responded.

"Everyone's waiting for you. Please come this way."

Jim waved for Mom and Dad to join him.

"Do you know what you're doing?" Dad asked.

"Yes, just follow me and bring in the box," said Jimmy.

Jimmy's father carried in a large box with Yankee pinstripes. It was the same box he had brought A1-33 home in, eleven years earlier.

Jimmy and his parents entered into a large conference room. Sitting around the table was Mr. Tansey, the scout who issued Jim the summer contract with the Instructional League. Additionally, Billy Martin, the ex-Yankee player and now team manager was there. Entering from a rear door was Mr. Steinbrenner, President and General Manager of the New York Yankees.

Everyone looked at Jim, and then at his father holding a large box with Yankee pinstripes. Jim wished he could read their minds. They must have thought the McNeil family was completely nuts.

Mr. Tansey had everyone take their seats, and then went through introductions.

Mr. Steinbrenner began to speak, "You know, Jim, no one has ever advanced from the Instructional League directly into the majors in the history of our organization. With the World Series beginning tomorrow, I sure hope everything I hear about you is true."

Jimmy smiled. There was no way he was about to let down the New York Yankees!

"Your coach down in Florida says you're the best infielder he's ever seen," said Mr. Steinbrenner. "And from what I hear, you can even hit for power."

Jim felt a bit embarrassed as he thanked Mr. Steinbrenner for his supportive words.

"Mr. Tansey is going to present you with a standard contract for your signature," said Mr. Steinbrenner. "Besides an entry level salary, there's an additional $50,000 signing bonus."

Jim could hear his mom softly gasp as she heard the offer. He then reached across the table for the contract and quickly scanned through it.

Jim looked up at everyone within the Yankee organization, and shook his head no.

"No?" Mr. Steinbrenner asked. "Do you know what you're doing here, son? Don't blow this chance for yourself."

"I don't want the $50,000 bonus," Jim said.

"You don't want the money?" Mr. Steinbrenner asked.

"No, sir," Jim answered as he got up out of his chair. He went over to the box on the table. He then lifted the top off of it with the same joy and excitement he had eleven years earlier. Jim pulled A1-33 out of the box and placed him on the conference table.

"This is A1-33," Jim said. "It's a box seat that was removed during the remodeling of the stadium. My father was on the construction crew."

The three men looked at John McNeil, who just smiled back proudly.

"A1-33 was given to my dad by the foreman, because he was the only one who could unfasten the seat from the concrete," said Jim. "During its time, this was Mrs. Gehrig's box seat. As you know, Mr. Steinbrenner, all the seats were dismantled that year and sold piece by piece as memorabilia."

Mr. Steinbrenner stared intensely at A1-33.

"Well, I've had A1-33 since I was eleven-years-old," continued Jim. "Keep the $50,000, sir. But please, install A1-33 back to its original spot six rows behind the first base dugout."

"What a great idea," laughed Mr. Steinbrenner as he looked at everyone seated at the table. "What publicity! This is great. Now if we install the seat, you'll sign the contract?"

"No," Jim said.

"What?" yelled George Steinbrenner. "Listen, Jim, enough is enough. Do you want to be a Yankee or not?"

"Yes, sir, it's my life long dream."

"Then sign the contract," he insisted.

"One other thing."

George Steinbrenner sighed and again sat back in his seat.

"What do you want Jim?" Mr. Steinbrenner asked.

"There's a friend of mine who was an usher here for many years. He's also the greatest Yankee fan of all time, and I do mean of all time," said Jim. "If the series goes to seven games, the final game will be played here in New York. I want my friend, Sam to be at the game with A1-33."

George Steinbrenner looked up.

"Kid, you better be worth it!" he said.

CHAPTER 37

At the neighborhood diner, Larry Barnes spun on his counter stool. He looked over to see what all the commotion was about. At the corner end of the counter, three men were pointing excitedly to the back page of the *New York Post*.

Larry assumed they were talking about the World Series opener at Yankee Stadium. After all, the entire city was buzzing with excitement. He then turned back to his coffee and buttered roll.

"I remember him when he played in Little League," said one of the men.

Larry slowly looked back, and began to listen closely to the conversation.

"McNeil is not only a great ballplayer," said the man, "he also has heart. Can you imagine turning down 50,000 big ones, just so baseball history can be preserved?"

At this point, Larry Barnes got up from his seat and cautiously walked toward the group conversation. His eyes continuously focused on the back page of the newspaper. Once it was in clear view, Barnes froze in place.

The sports page headline read, "Yanks Sign Local Star."

Below the words, in a full page picture, Jim McNeil and George Steinbrenner were six rows behind the Yankee dugout, standing on each side of A1-33. The box seat had been repositioned into its old home.

Larry Barnes slumped down onto a counter stool, burying his head in his hands. The distraught look on his face soon caught everyone's attention. The diner fell silent. Suddenly, Larry heard a calm voice behind him.

"You know, it's not too late to change, Larry," the voice said. "You still have time."

Larry removed his hands from his face. Looking up, he immediately recognized Sam.

"But I never got a single break," said Larry.

"Everyone chooses which pitches to swing at in life. Larry, so far you've fished after the bad ones." You never let anybody help you realize your potential, You spend your energy fighting teamwork and the respect of others."

Larry looked directly into Sam's eyes without saying a word. Sam looked back, never changing the expression on his face. Sam then turned and silently left the diner. As Larry remained speechless, the conversation about Jim McNeil and The New York Yankees resumed. Larry quietly got up and began to leave.

"Hey Barnes!" shouted one of the diner customers.

Larry turned back and looked around.

"Weren't you on the same Little League All-Star team with McNeil back in '75?"

"Yes," Larry said quietly. "I mean, no. I played, but I was never on the team."

Confused by Larry's comment, the man said, "Too bad, 'cause you were a good ballplayer. They sure could've used you."

"I'm just beginning to realize that," Larry said as he walked out.

CHAPTER 38

Jim walked out of the Yankee dugout. It was game seven of the World Series, and it was the greatest day of his life. As he stepped onto the grass, he looked around the stadium. He was standing in the same spot he had been in many years ago.

Jim recalled sitting on a steel girder the day he went to work with his dad. Jim remembered how the stadium had been torn up. His Dad was right, though; Yankee Stadium became new and improved.

Jim looked up into the stands to see if he could find his family. Jillie had come home from college for the game. Jim knew the entire family was as excited as he was. He looked up toward A1-33. Standing in front of the seat was Sam, wearing a maroon blazer, blue pants, and a furry glove on his left hand. Sam walked toward him.

"Jim, you've made two friends very happy," said Sam. "We know you can win it for us today."

With a smile, Jim waved to Sam and A1-33. Billy Martin then called Jim back into the dugout.

The game began at precisely 8:05 p.m., and the following two and half-hours proved to be the toughest ball game Jim had ever played in. The Yankees were down one run in the bottom of the ninth, and time was quickly running out. Jim was hitting in the bottom of the order, even though his series average was .300.

Jim would be the fourth batter up, if he were lucky enough to get a turn. The leadoff batter walked, and, unless there was a double-play, Jim knew he was going to hit. The next two batters each flied out.

Jim came to bat for the Yanks, down one run in the bottom of the ninth, during the seventh game of the World Series.

As Jim took his stroll from the on-deck circle, he could hear the crowd cheering. That old nervous pit fell back into his stomach. Then he heard A1-33 say: "Just have fun, Jim. Remember, that's the purpose of the game."

The next thing Jim knew, he was standing at home plate. On the mound, the pitcher was staring him down. Before Jim stepped into the batter's box, he looked out and viewed the center field monuments behind the outfield fence. Jim glanced toward the runner on first.

Jim knew he had been here before, in this very time, in this very spot.

The umpire called for him to step up to the plate, and he did. The first pitch was a fastball on the inside corner. The umpire yelled, "Strike one."

Jim fouled the second pitch down the left field line for strike two. The next two pitches missed the strike zone, bringing the count to 2-2.

Jim knew quite clearly that the next pitch would be a waist high fastball on the outside corner. He dug his spikes into the ground, and re-gripped his bat. As the pitch came in, he kept his eyes on the ball and swung even. He watched as contact between the bat and the ball was made.

As Jim started to run, he saw the ball sailing into deep center field. The outfielder was angling back toward the ball. Both the fielder and the ball were getting closer to the fence. The outfielder's glove was going up and up as he leaped toward the ball, but he banged off the wall as the ball cleared the fence for a two-run homer.

Jimmy couldn't believe it. The Yankees had won the game and the World Series!

Throughout the stadium, Jim could hear the crowd going wild. He thought in disbelief, *I am the luckiest man on the face of the earth.*

As Jim rounded first and was heading for second, he stared directly into center field and realized the ball had landed in front of Lou Gehrig's monument. An instant flash of light expelled from the baseball great's engraved portrait. Jim raised his hand and ceremoniously tipped the beak of his helmet to all the monuments. For it is in their honor that baseball will always be remembered.

When baseball is no longer fun, it's no longer a game.

–Joe DiMaggio

I thought I would write to let you know that The Box Seat Dream has met with what I can only call your toughest critic – my 11-year old nephew, Michael. I gave him a copy to read on his family's return car trip to Missouri (from NJ) and I just spoke to him. He loved it!!! You have something special here with this book to make the likes of him sit quietly in a car for hours. My brother and sister-in-law thank you.

–Joe Wedick

The book is great. I have read it and so has my daughter. We both loved It.

–Candy Bailey, President, Parkview Little League, California

It is so often difficult to find books that have enough realistic adventure to lure students to read. The Box Seat Dream is the perfect blend of fun and fantasy.

–Deborah Hinrichs, 5th Grade Schoolteacher, Massachusetts

The life lessons in The Box Seat Dream are those I teach all my students and athletes. I appreciate the story's emphasis on sportsmanship and the intense competition found in every game. I really thought I was at the ballpark.

–Sandrine Krul, Athletic Director & Teacher, Guardian Angel School

The Box Seat Dream is an exciting sports story that identifies the real life obstacles confronted by children athletes as they learn to compete, excel, and play in a teamwork environment. I wish I had read this as a child.

–Denis Herron, former NHL player with the Montreal Canadians and Pittsburgh Penguins

The Box Seat Dream is a timeless baseball fantasy for the entire family. This bedtime classic accurately describes the feel, smell and touch of growing up with baseball.

–Phillip Apreda, Officer, Southern Little League, Teaneck, New Jersey